DON'T CRY DARLING

The DI Jack Knox mysteries Book 7

ROBERT McNEILL

Published by The Book Folks, London, 2023

Mass market paperback, 2025

ISBN 978-1-80462-144-8

www.thebookfolks.com

This book is the seventh to feature DI Jack Knox. Details about the other novels can be found at the end of this one.

A list of characters featured in this book can also be found at the back.

Chapter One

The three men never heard their killer approach. The gunman padded softly upstairs, where a crack of light cut across the carpet from a room on the first-floor landing.

His targets were seated at a plain wooden table. All had cigarettes on the go, creating a pall of smoke which wreathed an unshaded bulb hanging from the ceiling.

One of the trio, a muscular individual in his mid-forties, took a pack of cards from the table and glanced at the others. 'My turn to deal, I think,' he said.

'Right,' replied the sallow-faced man on his left. He smiled and added, 'No flipping from the bottom now, Rab.'

The man shot him an indignant look. 'When have you ever caught me cheating?'

This caused the third player, a man with bushy eyebrows, to snort loudly. He nudged his pale-faced companion and said, 'Aye, that's the thing – eh, Billy? Not been caught *yet*, has he?'

Rab gave him an icy stare. 'Tam,' he said, 'if I thought for a minute you were serious...'

The assassin, now standing immediately outside the room, reached into his jacket and retrieved a Beretta M9 from a shoulder holster. He threaded a suppressor silently onto the muzzle, and made ready.

Inside, as Rab began to deal, Tam extended his hands in a mollifying gesture. 'Come on, Rab,' he said, 'you know I was only kidding.' A few seconds passed. 'By the way, you remember Alfie White, the scam artist? Now he *was* one to watch. One time at a poker game in Gorgie he had the entire deck marked. Way he worked it was—'

Tam was shocked into silence by the door, which suddenly flew open.

A moment later the shooter entered, took aim, and fired twice.

His first bullet hit the dealer, who dropped to the floor, blood spurting from a carotid artery.

Tam was the next man targeted. The bullet connected a few millimetres above the bridge of his nose and he too collapsed, blood and brain matter pooling onto the parquet from a hole in his forehead.

The man called Billy looked aghast as he saw the Beretta's muzzle was pointed at him.

'N– no,' he sputtered. 'For Christ's sake. Please.'

The gunman regarded him dispassionately, then nodded to an empty chair at the head of the table.

'Leckie,' he said. 'Your boss. Where is he?'

'Sh– Shug?'

'Uh-huh, Shug. Where is he?'

'F– Falkirk.'

'Falkirk?'

'Aye. He had to pull out at the last minute. His mother had a stroke. She's been taken to hospital.' Billy gave his questioner a beseeching look and added, 'Listen, pal, I'm only his caretaker. I think you're making a mis–'

There was a dull *thunk* as the Beretta was triggered a third time, and moments later Billy lay prostrate alongside his companions.

His executioner walked slowly around the table, making sure all three of his victims were dead, and came upon the empty chair. 'Bastard,' he said, giving it a kick that sent it spinning across the room. 'Damn bastard.'

* * *

'So Olivia alighted the last tram at the National Gallery at twenty past eleven on Friday, 14 April,' Marcus Ledbetter was asking. 'The onboard CCTV confirms this?'

Ledbetter, a tall man in late middle age, had a patrician look and spoke in an authoritarian manner.

Detective Inspector Jack Knox checked his notebook. 'Yes, sir,' he confirmed. 'We also obtained CCTV images from two department stores and a hotel. Your daughter Olivia can be seen walking along Princes Street afterwards, turning right onto Waverley Bridge.'

Ledbetter nodded. 'She would have been heading back to her flat in Jeffrey Street.'

His wife, Eloise, took a hankie from her handbag and dabbed her eyes. 'But never arrived,' she said.

Knox glanced at her. She was a petite woman with high cheekbones and raven-black hair, and looked to be a decade younger than her husband.

He flicked over a page of his notebook again and said, 'Okay, just to recap: Emma, your eighteen-year-old youngest daughter, had been staying with Olivia at her flat in Edinburgh since Sunday, 9 April. They had dinner at the Cafe Royal in West Register Street on the last day of Emma's visit, and took a tram to the airport. Olivia saw her sister off on the ten o'clock flight, then caught the last tram back to town?'

Marcus Ledbetter nodded. 'Yes. Eloise and I met Emma at Heathrow and drove her home. Just before twelve we phoned Olivia to confirm her sister had arrived safely, but the call went straight to voicemail–'

'Which is strange,' his wife interrupted. 'Olivia doesn't normally switch off her mobile.'

Ledbetter nodded. 'Her flatmate answered the landline when we checked with her. She confirmed Olivia hadn't arrived.'

Knox was accompanied by DS Bill Fulton, a stocky man in his mid-fifties. The sergeant leaned forward in his chair and asked, 'What time would that have been, sir?'

Ledbetter gave his wife an inquiring look. 'Around twelve-fifteen, wouldn't you say, dear?'

Eloise Ledbetter dabbed her eyes again. 'Yes.'

Knox nodded. 'How long has your daughter been staying there?'

Eloise unclipped her handbag and replaced the hankie. 'About seven weeks,' she said. 'Olivia moved in late February, just after her twenty-first birthday.'

Ledbetter straightened and his chair protested noisily. 'Ms Fiona Douglas, the young lady with whom my daughter stays, has been unable to shine a light on Olivia's disappearance. Said she didn't know her that well.'

'You spoke to Ms Douglas?' Knox asked.

'Only on the telephone.'

'They're not friends?' Fulton asked.

Eloise shook her head. 'Not really. It's simply a sharing arrangement. My daughter met Ms Douglas when she advertised the flat in a local newspaper. The property's a three-room apartment, furnished. Olivia has one bedroom, Ms Douglas the other. The sitting room, kitchen and bathroom are shared.'

Knox thought for a moment or two, then said, 'Isn't it possible Olivia met someone – a boyfriend, perhaps, or someone she knows from work?'

Ledbetter's face turned a deep shade of crimson, and his voice rose an octave. 'Buggered off without letting anyone know, you mean? Particularly myself and Eloise – whom she knew would almost certainly ring to let her know we'd met her sister? Olivia's mobile was *off*, Detective Inspector.' He glared at Knox and added, 'Good God, man; you *are* taking my daughter's disappearance seriously?'

'Marcus, *please*,' his wife said, 'keep your temper – the officer is only trying to help.'

Ledbetter composed himself, and a few moments later he spoke again. 'I'm sorry,' he said gruffly.

'It's okay, sir,' Knox replied. 'I understand your concern. But we must consider every possibility.' He turned to Eloise and continued, '*Was* your daughter seeing anyone, Mrs Ledbetter, do you know?'

'Perhaps,' she replied, then shook her head and added, 'it's something we never discussed.'

'I see,' Knox said, and consulted his notes. 'Olivia works as a trainee at the solicitors Fairbairn and Millar, in Abercromby Place?'

'Yes,' Mrs Ledbetter said. 'She started in March, two weeks after she arrived in Edinburgh. We contacted the firm yesterday and spoke to a Ms Breadlove, their administrator. She told us Olivia had arranged for a period of leave while her sister was in the city.'

'When was she due to start back?' Knox asked.

'Tomorrow.'

'Wednesday the 19th?' Knox asked.

'Yes.'

'So it's possible she may yet resume her duties?'

'Well, I–'

Again her husband became animated. He leaned forward in his chair and interrupted his wife. 'Look here,' he said. 'Olivia's silence over the weekend and the fact she hasn't returned to her flat make us think that highly unlikely. You're wasting time, man. You have to do something *now*.'

Knox nodded. 'We're taking your daughter's disappearance seriously, Mr Ledbetter,' he said and tapped his notebook. 'We'll interview her flatmate, then speak to Olivia's colleagues at Fairbairn and Millar. I'm confident we'll come up with something.' He rose, and Fulton followed his lead. 'You and Mrs Ledbetter will be staying here at the Carlton?'

'Of course,' Ledbetter said emphatically. 'Until we discover our daughter's whereabouts.'

'Fine,' Knox said, and gave his wife a reassuring smile. 'I wouldn't worry. It's very likely some sort of misunderstanding.'

* * *

'Arrogant bugger, isn't he?' Fulton was saying as he and Knox exited the hotel and got into the DI's car. 'The lassie's only been incommunicado for a day or two. It stands to reason, if she doesn't start back till tomorrow. Like you suggested, boss — she'll be shacked up with a boyfriend somewhere. Forgotten to charge her mobile too, most likely.'

Knox shrugged. 'Maybe,' he said. 'But her silence does appear unusual. Might be more to it.'

'Aye, boss,' Fulton said, 'there might.' He shook his head and added, 'What I can't understand though is why they've given it to us. Why not kick it over to uniform? Normal procedure in a misper case.'

A faint smile played on Knox's lips. 'Influence,' he said.

'Influence?' Fulton echoed.

'Aye,' Knox said. 'Warburton told me the job came from Gartcosh.'

'Ah,' Fulton said. 'Friends in high places.'

Knox nodded. 'Uh-huh. Apparently Ledbetter and the ACC are close pals.'

Fulton gave Knox a sardonic look. 'Same handshake?'

'Wouldn't rule it out.'

Knox's iPhone rang at that moment and he took the device from his pocket, placed it on a dash mount, and switched to the car's speakers. 'Knox,' he said.

'Jack,' said the voice at the other end of the line. 'You've spoken to Ledbetter?'

DCI Ronald Warburton, Knox's boss, was calling from Gayfield Square, the station where the detectives were based. Warburton had phoned him at home earlier, briefed him on Olivia's disappearance, and asked him to talk to her parents at the Carlton Hotel. 'Yes, sir,' he said. 'Bill and I have concluded our interview.'

'Any leads?'

'One or two possibles,' Knox replied. 'Olivia's room-mate and the solicitor's office where she works. Might get a handle on her movements if we speak to the flat-share girl and Olivia's co-workers.'

'Can you pass that over to McCann and Hathaway?' Warburton said. 'They're both here.'

Knox checked his watch: 9.10am. DS Arlene McCann and DC Mark Hathaway were the two other officers on his team, and would have recently arrived at the office.

'Something's up?' Knox said, frowning.

'Afraid so, Jack,' Warburton said. '101 Spylaw Road, Merchiston. Triple homicide. A pistol appears to have been the murder weapon.'

It took a moment or two for Knox to absorb this information, then the speakers crackled again. 'Jack,' Warburton said. 'You still there?'

'Sir,' Knox replied. 'The forensic team's at the scene?'

'Yes,' Warburton said. 'DI Murray and his assistant, DS Beattie. The pathologist, too.'

'Lucy Carmichael?'

'No, I hear she's in the States for a few weeks. Alex Turley's standing in for her.'

'Sir,' Knox replied. A pause, then, 'Spylaw Road – isn't that where Hugh Leckie lives?'

'The George Street security deposit thief turned property magnate?' Warburton replied, adding, 'Yes, I believe so.'

'He was one of the men shot?'

'I really don't know,' Warburton replied. 'You'll head over there?'

Knox turned the starter and the Passat's engine fired. 'We're on our way now, sir,' he said.

Chapter Two

Knox dialled DS McCann's number and a few seconds later her voice came over the speakers.

'Morning, boss,' she said.

'Morning, Arlene,' Knox replied. 'Warburton's spoken to you?'

'Yes,' McCann replied. 'He told us you and Bill were interviewing a couple in connection with their daughter's disappearance. Said the request for CID involvement had come from Gartcosh. It's pretty high profile?'

'They're friends of the ACC,' Knox said.

'Ah,' McCann said. 'That would explain it.'

'Warburton say anything about Merchiston?'

'The three men shot? Yeah, we heard, but not from the chief. Danny on the desk told us when we arrived.'

Knox steered the Passat around a bus, whose indicators came on at the last minute as it drew into a stop. 'Right,' he said. 'Well, Warburton wants Bill and I to head over to Spylaw Road. Asked for you and Mark to carry on with the Ledbetter case in the meantime. Got a notebook handy?'

A couple of seconds passed, and McCann replied, 'I have now, boss. Fire away.'

Knox relayed the gist of the interview with the Ledbetters, brought the DS up to date on Olivia's roommate, and told her about Olivia's position at Fairbairn and Millar.

'You can check HOLMES 2 on your desktop for Olivia's file and photograph,' he concluded. 'Together with CCTV clips.'

'You want us to see Fiona Douglas first?'

'Probably,' Knox replied. 'Since she's likely to know Olivia better. Might be an idea to give her a ring before you leave, though,' he added. 'Make sure she's at home.'

'Okay, boss,' McCann said. 'We'll get to it. Keep you posted.'

* * *

'Known as Writer's Block, this area,' Fulton was saying. He and Knox had driven up through Bruntsfield and turned into Merchiston Place. 'Ian Rankin, Alexander McCall Smith, J K Rowling, all live within shouting distance of each other. Or at least they used to.'

Knox grinned. 'Really? Never took you for a literary buff, Bill.'

Fulton looked slightly abashed. 'Who, me?' he replied. 'Nah, it's the wife and grandkids. She reads McCall Smith's *Ladies' Detective Agency* stories and my daughter's kids love Harry Potter.'

'And the Rebus fan, that's you?' Knox asked.

'Aye, I admit. I've read one or two. They're not bad.'

'You said the novelists *used* to live in Merchiston. That's no longer the case?'

'McCall Smith still does, I think. The other two moved. J K Rowling stays in Barnton now. Rankin flitted to Quartermile, in Lauriston Place.'

The detectives lapsed into silence for several moments, then Fulton spoke again, 'Hugh Leckie's place is fairly impressive, too, I've been told. When did the George Street robbery take place?'

'It was 2003,' Knox replied. 'The gang's trial was a year later. Leckie was sentenced to twelve years, served eight.'

'Weren't you on the case?'

'Yes, based at St Leonards. I'd just been promoted DI.'

'Whose collar was it?' Fulton asked.

'DCI Ron Fletcher.'

'Aye,' Fulton said, 'I remember. Didn't one of the gang's brothers blow the whistle?'

'Andy O'Dowd. Played a minor part in the raid; wasn't happy with his cut when the proceeds were divvied up.'

'Fletch conducted his interview?' Fulton asked.

'Yeah.'

Fulton grinned. 'Aye, word is he gave no quarter. O'Dowd squealed in fairly short order.'

'Andy had an aversion to doing time,' Knox replied. 'The idea of a lengthy prison sentence didn't sit well with him. Fletcher threatened fifteen years – as opposed to eighteen months if he cooperated fully.'

'Didn't he name his brother?'

'Aye, Charlie. The other three were Tommy Salter, Norman McVey, and Leckie.'

'Wasn't the raid similar to the Hatton Garden job in 2015?' Fulton asked.

'Pretty much,' Knox said. 'Except it wasn't done in two stages over a long weekend, but in one night, middle of the week.'

'But they got away with a fair haul?'

'Yeah, an estimated five million in cash, gold and diamonds. Not as impressive as the fourteen mil in London, but a tidy sum nonetheless.'

'And there's a fair bit unrecovered, if memory serves,' Fulton said.

'Yes,' Knox replied. 'A couple of million, maybe more. A cache of diamonds.'

'Aye, I remember hearing that. Part of a collection belonging to an Arab sheikh?'

'Yes, the owner's located in Qatar. A DC Mitchell and myself interviewed his agent. The man confirmed that a box of gems were missing.'

Fulton blew out his cheeks. 'Not hard to imagine where Leckie got the money to start his property business,' he said.

Knox nodded, 'I'm inclined to agree. Leckie owns a string of houses and flats, all in the better areas; Blackhall, Buckstone, Craiglockhart – and here in Merchiston. Yet when he was investigated by the Organised Crime Squad a couple of years back, they gave him a clean sheet. He was able to prove the seed money had been left to him by a relative. Told them he'd started by buying ex-council houses, did a bit of renovation, and sold them on. They went over his books and found nothing untoward.'

'Mm-hmm,' Fulton said. 'He might be one of the three men shot?'

Knox shrugged and nodded ahead. 'We'll find out shortly,' he replied.

Knox turned into the driveway of a two-storey sandstone villa set back off the road and pulled up at the entrance. A young constable stood watch in front of a double front door sheltered by a pillared porch.

The detectives exited and Knox showed the man his warrant card. 'DI Knox and DS Fulton,' he said. 'The forensic officers and pathologist – they're inside?'

The officer thumbed over his shoulder. 'Up the stairway on your left, sir,' he said. 'Second room on the first-floor landing.'

'Okay, Bill,' Knox said, nodding to the Passat's boot. 'You and I better put on our protective gear and join them.'

* * *

'All three were shot in the head or neck,' the pathologist was saying.

Knox and Fulton were in the room where the killings had taken place, the men's corpses still in situ. Alexander Turley was on his knees, using a penlight to examine the neck of the last man.

Forensic officers DI Ed Murray and DS Liz Beattie stood nearby, Murray checking the screen of a camera, Beattie using a UV lamp to look for footprints. Murray was in his late forties, around the same age as Knox; Beattie a decade or more younger.

Murray let the camera dangle from its strap for a moment, and indicated the pathologist. 'Alex just dug out a bullet, 9mm Parabellum,' he said. 'And we found three cartridge cases. Narrows the make of weapon used. Most likely an automatic: Beretta, SIG Sauer or Glock.'

Turley nodded. 'The bullet went right through to the back of his neck,' he explained, moving the penlight to illuminate a gaping wound at the front. 'Entered here, severing the carotid artery, only just missed his cervical vertebrae, after which it partially exited the splenius capitis – one of the big muscles at the back of the neck. I'll extract the bullets from the other two when I carry out their post-mortems.'

'Who found them?' Knox asked.

'A postie saw the front door ajar,' Murray replied. 'The gunman must have left in a hurry. Royal Mail passed it on and a local patrol checked.'

Knox dipped his head in acknowledgement and indicated the victims. 'Who are they, do we know?' he asked.

'We found ID in their pockets,' Beattie said. 'The guy with Alex is William Copeley. The driving licence gives his address as 33 Admiralty Street, Leith. Date of birth, 12 March 1980, which makes him forty-three.

'The other two are Thomas Reilly – his licence puts his age at forty-seven, lived at 93 Bath Street, Portobello; and Robert Scott, we unearthed a bank statement addressed to him at 84 Wardlaw Street, Gorgie, he looks to be in his early fifties.'

Knox nodded. 'You were able to confirm the property still belongs to Hugh Leckie?'

'It appears so,' Murray said. 'Liz found a couple of recent bills on a ledge near the entrance. One from BT, the other from Scottish Power. I can check the property register later to confirm.'

Fulton gestured to the dead men. 'These lads must be known to him,' he said.

'Looks that way,' Knox said, and glanced around the room, which was empty of furniture save for a table and four chairs. A number of playing cards were scattered over the parquet-tiled floor. One of the chairs lay on its side near the window.

'Very likely the shooter surprised them in the middle of a card game,' Murray said.

'Aye,' Knox replied, and pointed to the fallen chair. 'It was like that when you came in?'

'On its side?' Murray said. 'Yeah, exactly. Nothing's been moved, Jack. You know procedure.'

'I know, Ed, I know,' Knox said. 'Just making sure.' He paused. 'Leckie's property, but no Leckie. Four chairs and a table but nothing else. Couldn't help but notice other rooms in the house are empty of furniture, too. I wonder why?'

'Maybe he's moving out?' Fulton said.

Beattie shook her head. 'Didn't see any for-sale signs when we came in,' she said.

Knox nodded. 'You're right, Liz,' he said. 'Neither did we. Perhaps he hasn't got around to putting it on the market.'

'Maybe Leckie was to have made a fourth at bridge, or whatever game they were playing,' Fulton said. 'Didn't turn up for some reason.'

Knox's eyes widened. 'You're right, Bill. Why didn't I think of that?'

Fulton smiled. 'Why we're a team, boss,' he said.

Knox returned an acknowledging grin. 'That chair's a good ten feet from the others,' he said. 'And likely to have been moved *after* they were shot.'

Turley stood suddenly, a task which appeared to cause him difficulty. 'Ooh,' he said, placing a hand on the small of his back. 'They say old age doesn't come alone,' he added. 'Too damned true.'

'Come on, Alex,' Beattie said, smiling. 'What are you, fifty-nine? Still a young man.'

'Sixty-three and retired,' Turley replied. 'Or supposed to be. Lucy Carmichael can't get back quick enough.'

'DCI Warburton tells us she's in the USA?' Fulton said.

'Aye, for a month. Quantico, Virginia. On an exchange visit with the FBI's forensics department. Her American counterpart is at Gartcosh.' He shot Knox a wry look. 'I thought your boss would've known that.'

Knox met Turley's gaze, gave a thin smile, and said, 'We're not as close as you'd like to believe, Alex.'

'No tales out of school, eh?' Turley replied, grinning, then gestured towards Copeley's body. 'Anyway, your supposition on the course of events: take a look at the hands of our friend here.'

Knox did so. 'They're extended?' he said.

'Exactly,' Turley replied. 'Any idea why?'

Knox considered this for a moment. 'He knew he was about to be shot; an automatic reflex?'

Turley indicated the bodies of the other two men. 'Precisely. My theory concurs with yours and Ed's – the group were taken by surprise. Reilly and Scott had no time to react; never knew what hit them. Copeley, on the other hand, had words with the gunman.'

'Of course,' Knox exclaimed, pointing towards the top of the table. 'The shooter was after Leckie, who'd have been seated there... He quizzed Copeley about Leckie's whereabouts, didn't like the answer, then triggered the kill shot and took his anger out on the chair – kicked it across the room.'

'As good a supposition as any, Jack,' Turley said.

'How did the murdered men get here, though?' Fulton asked. 'No car outside.'

'Leckie dropped them off,' Knox said. 'I'm guessing the card game's a regular thing – every Monday, maybe.' Knox's brow furrowed, and he added, 'Something came up and Leckie had to leave. The shooter arrives an hour or so later, enters by a door or window – the place is almost empty, so security's not an issue – makes his way upstairs and carries out the killings.'

Murray gestured to the chair. 'Well, if he came into contact with the chair, there's a fair chance of us finding an impression of a shoe or boot. Naturally, Liz and I are paying special attention to this room.'

Turley picked up his medical bag. 'Well, if you folks have no objection, I'm heading off. I phoned my assistants twenty minutes ago and they'll be here any minute to pick up the bodies.'

'I can check with you later, Alex, after you've completed the PMs?' Knox asked.

'Aye, any time after three, Jack,' Turley replied. 'I'll be able to confirm time and cause of death.'

Knox nodded, and pointed to the body of the man Turley had just examined. 'Fine, Alex,' he said. 'And thanks for your insights on how Copeley died.'

'Any time, Jack,' Turley said. 'All part of the service.'

As the pathologist left the room, Knox turned to Beattie. 'The BT bill found near the entrance, Liz,' he said. 'You've still got it?'

'Sure, boss,' Beattie said. She extracted an envelope from her carry-case and gave it to him.

'Thanks,' Knox said, he removed the bill and studied it for a moment. 'Yes!' he exclaimed.

'What?' Fulton asked.

'Leckie's mobile,' Knox replied. 'It's on the same contract as his landline. 'I've got the number here.'

Chapter Three

DS McCann found a vacant bay overlooking Waverley Station. She parked the Astra, then she and Hathaway exited and headed back along Jeffrey Street.

'Number thirty-seven?' the young detective asked when they arrived at a row of shops.

'Yeah, second floor,' McCann replied.

'Got it,' Hathaway said, pointing a finger at the list of occupants alongside the entry system at a door between a café and a leather goods shop. 'Here we are,' he added. 'Ms Fiona Douglas.'

'Better let me,' McCann said.

Hathaway stood to one side, and she pressed the button. A few moments later a woman's voice came over the intercom. 'Yes?'

'Ms Douglas? It's DS Arlene McCann – we spoke on the phone?'

'Oh, yes,' Douglas replied. 'Come on up.'

A buzzer sounded, and the detectives entered and ascended to the second floor.

Fiona Douglas was waiting at the far side of the landing. She was a slim, dark-haired woman in her late twenties and was wearing a dressing gown. Gesturing to the hallway behind her, she said, 'The living room's along on the left. Please, come in and take a seat on the settee. I've just made coffee. Would you like a cup?'

'No, thanks,' McCann said. 'We had some before we left the office.'

Douglas showed the detectives into the living room, after which she departed for the kitchen, reappearing a minute later carrying a mug of coffee.

She sat on an armchair opposite and held the mug on her lap. 'You still haven't heard from Olivia?' she said earnestly.

'Unfortunately, no,' McCann replied. 'Our colleagues interviewed her parents this morning. They said they'd spoken to you.'

'Yes,' Douglas said. 'They phoned me twice. Just after midnight early Sunday, and again yesterday.'

McCann nodded. 'They mentioned that Olivia moved into the flat with you in February?'

'Yes, Wednesday the 22nd to be precise,' Douglas replied. 'I made a note on the calendar.' After a pause, he continued, 'Olivia got in touch after I advertised in the *Evening News*. The agency who manage the flat told me the owners were raising rents at the beginning of 2023. I couldn't continue to lease the place on my own.'

'How long have you been a tenant?' Hathaway asked.

'Since March, 2020. I moved in just as the coronavirus pandemic began. I could afford the rent as at the time I managed a hairdressing salon. But when Covid spread, the lockdowns began to have an impact. The salon's owner was forced to lay off some of the staff. I only survived by taking a cut in wages.'

'You're still a hairdresser?' McCann asked.

Douglas shook her head. 'No, unfortunately the salon closed in 2021. I was lucky, though. One of our customers advised of a job going at Craigentinny depot, cleaning trains. It's a night shift, but the pay's okay. I work Sunday to Thursday. Friday and Saturday nights off.'

McCann nodded. 'So, how well do you know Olivia?'

'Not that well, particularly with me working nights. I see her mostly in the evenings when she gets home from work. We often watch telly together for a few hours. Usually I'm heading out when she's getting ready for bed.'

'Has she told you much about herself?' McCann asked.

'Only that she was brought up by her parents in Bromley in Kent. Came up to Scotland on holiday in 2017, when she was fifteen, and liked it so much that she enrolled in St Andrews University three years later. She studied Scots law, and is currently doing a diploma in legal practice at the firm where she works.'

'Fairbairn and Millar, in Abercromby Place?' McCann asked.

'Yes,' Douglas replied.

'What about social life?'

'Boyfriends, you mean?'

'Yes.'

Douglas took a long sip of coffee. 'Well, I don't think she's seeing anyone at the moment. But she did tell me about a guy she'd been out on a date with just before she left university.' She shook her head and added, 'Olivia didn't like him much, described him as "clingy".'

'She told you his name?' McCann asked.

Douglas shook her head. 'No. And I didn't ask.'

'And has Olivia behaved any differently in the last week or so?'

Douglas studied McCann for a long moment. 'I'm not sure what you mean.'

'Has she appeared worried, or stressed?'

'No. Quite the opposite. She was delighted to be reunited with her sister for a few days. Told me she was looking forward to showing her the town.'

'Emma arrived on the 9th, a Sunday?'

'Yes,' Douglas said. 'Olivia was going to book her into a hotel, but I told her not to be daft, Emma could sleep here on the divan. It's a sofa bed.'

'And you last spoke to Olivia on Friday, the night she saw her sister off?' McCann asked.

'Yes,' Douglas replied. 'She and Emma had a 7pm reservation at the Cafe Royal. Olivia said they'd take a tram to the airport and she'd be back after eleven. I told her I'd probably be in bed, as I was dog tired – I've a helluva time adjusting after five days on night shift. I hit the hay after we said goodbye and heard nothing more until the phone rang just after midnight.'

'Her parents?' Hathaway said.

'Yes.'

'Olivia didn't say anything about meeting anyone after she saw her sister off?' McCann asked.

'No. As I told her parents, and the girl from her office when they rang, Olivia said she'd be back after eleven.'

'A girl from her office phoned you?'

'Uh-huh, just after 4pm yesterday,' Douglas said. 'A colleague called Wendy. Said she was ringing to check if Olivia was okay.'

'You told her Olivia was still missing?' McCann said.

'Yes.'

'What did she say in reply?'

'Just that she was concerned. She asked if Olivia had said anything about Grossman.'

'Grossman?'

'Yes. I asked her who Grossman was.'

'And?'

'If I remember correctly there was a bit of a silence, then she said, "Oh, don't worry, it's not that important," and hung up.'

* * *

Knox copied the mobile's number into his notebook and handed the BT envelope back to Beattie. 'Thanks, Liz,' he said. 'No doubt you'll want to check this.'

'Yes, we'll run it for prints along with other forensics.' She pointed to the floor, which minutes before she'd been sweeping with a UV scanner. 'Quite a number of footprints on the parquet tiles, which we'll cross-check with the men's footwear.'

Murray chimed in. 'Yes, more than likely we'll be able to isolate the shooter's prints.' He indicated the envelope Beattie was holding. 'He could have picked that up too at some point. Might find dabs on it.'

'Okay, Ed,' Knox said, and nodded to his colleague. 'Liz, we'll get out of your hair and leave you to it.'

Murray checked his watch. 'Photography and video's pretty much done, Jack; we should be able to finalise after Turley's assistants have picked up the bodies. We'll ring later, let you know if we find anything.'

Knox thanked the forensic officers, then he and Fulton exited the house and got back into the car. Knox placed his iPhone on the dash mount, checked his notebook, and keyed in the number he'd obtained from the BT bill.

Moments later a voice answered. 'Hello?'

'Mr Hugh Leckie?' Knox asked.

'Aye, who's that?'

'Detective Inspector Knox, Mr Leckie.'

'Police?' Leckie said cautiously. 'Something's wrong?'

Knox ignored the question. 'Mr Leckie,' he said, 'could you confirm you're the owner of a property situated at 101, Spylaw Road?'

'Aye,' Leckie replied hesitantly. 'I am.'

'And are you acquainted with three men called William Copeley, Thomas Reilly and Robert Scott?'

'Billy, Tam and Rab?' Leckie said. 'Aye, they work for me. Why do you ask?'

'Because all three were found shot dead in a first-floor room of your property at just after 8am this morning.'

The detectives heard a sharp intake of breath, then the line went silent.

'Mr Leckie,' Knox said. 'You still there?'

A moment or two passed, then, 'Shot dead, you say?'

'Yes, Mr Leckie,' Knox replied. 'All three.'

'For Christ's sake,' Leckie replied. 'Who'd do that?'

'Exactly what we'd like to find out,' Knox said.

'They were on the first floor, you say – a room with only one table and four chairs?' Leckie asked. 'Playing cards?'

'Yes,' Knox replied. 'Look, Mr Leckie, I'd like to speak to you face-to-face. Could you tell me where you are, please?'

'The Travelodge hotel in Falkirk,' Leckie replied. 'My mother lives in the town; she had a stroke yesterday afternoon. She's made a slight improvement, but I want to be handy, just in case.'

'I understand,' Knox said. 'Would it be possible for us to see you there? I understand your concerns for your mother, but you'll appreciate these murders are serious – we have to talk to you.'

'Yeah… all right.'

Knox checked his watch. 'My colleague and I can be with you in forty minutes: say eleven-thirty?'

'Aye, that'll be okay. I told the ward staff I'd be back to see her this afternoon, though.'

'We won't keep you any longer than necessary,' Knox replied.

* * *

'I was to have been there,' Leckie was saying. 'Playing poker. Got a call from the Forth Valley Hospital an hour before I was due to join them.'

He, Knox and Fulton were sitting at a table in the far corner of the Travelodge's lounge, which was empty save for an elderly couple sitting near the door. Leckie was short and stocky, and wore a heavy beard which was almost grey.

'The game's a fixture?' Fulton asked.

'Eh?' Leckie said distractedly.

'You and the men – playing cards on Mondays?'

'Oh, I see. Aye, it is.'

'The property's for sale?' Knox asked.

'Not yet,' Leckie replied. 'I'm converting it into flats. Waiting on renovation quotes from the builders.'

'And you were on your way to Spylaw Road when the hospital called you?'

'Yeah,' Leckie replied. 'I'd picked up the lads and was heading over. Dropped them off and told them to start the game without me.'

'You didn't see anything unusual when you arrived?'

Leckie shrugged. 'No, nothing.'

'The men,' Knox said. 'You said they worked for you – in what capacity?'

'All my properties are rented,' Leckie replied. 'The guys looked after the maintenance work. Tam is– was a plumber, Rab a spark and Billy a general handyman.'

Knox studied Leckie for a long moment. 'Did any of them have a prison record?' he said.

Leckie grimaced. 'Did I know them when I was inside, you mean?'

'Yes.'

Leckie shook his head. 'No. They'd done time, but not with me.' He gave Knox a pointed stare, and added, 'No doubt you've checked my record, Inspector. You're aware I was released in 2012.'

Knox nodded and continued, 'Had they any enemies you know of?'

Leckie shrugged. 'None I can think of who'd want to kill them – or me, come to that.'

'What about Andy O'Dowd?' Knox said.

'What about him?'

'The George Street CincScot Security company theft back in 2003,' Knox said. 'It's known he wasn't happy with his cut. Equally well known that his statement led to your arrest and that of your accomplices.'

Leckie gave a snort of derision. 'You're not up to date, are you? O'Dowd went to meet his maker three years ago… cancer.'

'I didn't know that,' Knox said. 'What about his brother, Charlie? Or McVey, or Salter?'

'Haven't seen them in years,' Leckie said. 'And why should they bear me a grudge? The three of us were given similar sentences. The loot was recovered.'

'Was it?' Knox said. 'I seem to recall a box of diamonds is missing.'

Leckie gave a stifled laugh. 'The Arab's jewels, you mean? Bit of a fairy tale, that one. You're forgetting the loot was stashed at my place, where it was divvied. There was no other box.'

'Could be someone doesn't believe that's the case,' Knox said.

'Then that's their bad luck, isn't it?' Leckie replied.

'Might have been bad luck for you, too, if you'd been in the card game,' Fulton said.

Leckie glared at the detective sergeant, but said nothing.

'You've a place to go to?' Knox said. 'That no one knows about?'

'You really think I was the target?' Leckie replied. 'Not a burglar the lads surprised?'

'What do you think, Mr Leckie?' Knox said.

'Aye,' Leckie said grimly. 'You're probably right.' He paused. 'I've a place at the Colonies in Stockbridge, bought last month; it's lying empty.'

'Then I suggest you relocate there for a while,' Knox said. 'We'll investigate meantime, keep you posted.'

Chapter Four

Olivia regained consciousness and, on opening her eyes, discovered she had double vision. Twin rectangles floated back and forth then, like the focus patch on a rangefinder camera, the images merged, and she realised she was looking at a television screen.

It took several moments to become fully aware of her surroundings.

She lay in an old-fashioned four-poster bed in a small room, a flat-screen television positioned on the wall facing her. It appeared to be tuned to a breakfast programme, a male and female presenter were seated on a red couch, holding a copy of a book and conversing with a middle-aged woman seated opposite. The sound had been muted, so Olivia couldn't hear what was being discussed.

Sunlight streamed through the slats of a venetian blind at a narrow window on Olivia's right. She turned her head in the opposite direction, and immediately felt giddy. The feeling subsided and she saw the room's entrance, a cream-painted door which almost matched the eggshell finish of the interior. The only other furniture was a dressing table situated opposite the window, and a ladderback chair placed near the door.

The bed had an old-fashioned look to it, as both head and footboards were made of metal. The outmoded theme continued with sheets and pillowcases, which were linen as opposed to cotton. She also realised it had been made up with blankets, rather than a duvet.

Olivia's attempt to raise her head was met with a second wave of giddiness, and she sank back into the pillows. She lay for a moment, straining her ears to detect any sound, but heard nothing.

Then, for the first time since coming to, she felt panic. Where the hell was she, how did she get here, and why did it feel like she'd been drugged?

Her thoughts went back to the previous evening.

It was the final day of Emma's visit and, as a special treat, she'd taken her sister to dinner at the Cafe Royal. Afterwards they'd made their way to St Andrew Square and boarded a tram for the airport. There they'd said goodbye, Emma promising to make sure that she or her parents would phone to let her know she'd arrived safely.

After the plane's departure, Olivia had boarded the last tram for Princes Street.

Whatever happened then, however, was shrouded in fog – a thick mist which appeared to have addled her brain.

She remembered a group of teenagers laughing, and two old women looking at her with disapproving expressions. She tried to recall what they were saying but their voices had sounded distant, as if in an echo chamber. She'd attempted to steady herself against something, and a man asked her a question. Then a car had stopped, and another man was talking to them. She thought he'd said something about being her fiancée. She'd tried to protest but couldn't get the words out. There was something familiar about this other man... suddenly his face came into focus: Clive Grossman! She'd tried to resist but he was leading her towards his car. She couldn't remember anything else after that.

Again Olivia took stock of her surroundings.

Oh my God, she thought. *If Clive Grossman brought me here, he must have put me to bed.*

She reached beneath the covers and discovered she was wearing a pair of men's pyjamas. Her knickers, bra and blouse appeared untouched. Only the skirt, cardigan, jacket and scarf worn the previous day were missing.

She didn't *feel* violated, but that didn't mean the bastard hadn't raped her.

Olivia took a deep breath. Grossman had been stalking her for months – why in the name of God hadn't she reported him?

It had all seemed so innocent in the beginning. They'd met during her first year at university. Grossman, a chemistry student, approached her in Market Street in St Andrews on a Saturday afternoon. She recognised him from one of the lecture theatres. He introduced himself and invited her for a drink.

Olivia had explained she was shopping, that there were several items she needed and couldn't put off buying.

'Later then,' he'd said, and she'd agreed.

He'd been pleasant enough at first – self-deprecating, with an almost childlike sense of humour. On the first date he told her that he'd been brought up by an aunt, as his father suffered from alcoholism and his mother was unable to cope.

He'd been introverted as a child and had few friends; his only interest through secondary school and college had been a passion for science. He told her he'd made up his mind to become an industrial chemist.

They went out again on a second date, which was when her interest began to wane. She realised he was more obsessed with himself than others, even to the extent of self-pity.

She discovered this when he asked to see her a third time. She had declined and he'd become morose, accusing her of seeing someone else. Olivia pointed out that she wasn't interested in forming a relationship at this time.

A few days later he'd called her on her mobile, apologised, and asked her to forgive him. Olivia had said there was nothing to forgive and reiterated her desire not to enter into a relationship.

'You'll come out with me once again, though, won't you?' he'd said. 'There's a new movie called *Reminiscence* showing at the New Picture House this week. Got quite good reviews. How about Saturday?'

'That's not a good idea, Clive,' she'd said.

'You're serious?' he'd said. 'You really don't want to go out with me?'

'I'm sorry, no.'

A short silence, then, 'There *is* someone else, isn't there?'

'Look, Clive,' she replied. 'I've already explained – and I don't want to discuss it further. Please, don't call me again.'

But he had. She couldn't prove it as the calls always came from public call boxes. Her response of 'Hello?' would be met with silence.

Soon afterwards she'd be walking in the grounds of the university or in the town of St Andrews when she'd have a feeling of someone following her. She'd turn and see him standing there, a hundred or so yards distant. He'd stare but say nothing, his face expressionless.

She'd shrugged it off and, when the calls and stalking took place on fewer occasions, she assumed he'd got the message.

Except that he hadn't. Soon, packages began to arrive. The first containing a silver brooch with a card that said, "Missing you, Olivia – your true love". In her last few months at St Andrews, several more arrived, always wrapped in plain brown paper with no return address. Sometimes they contained a bouquet of flowers, occasionally a box of chocolates. Always accompanied with an unsigned card which bore a similar message: "Still missing you, Olivia – your true love".

She always dumped the packages, and never discussed his unwanted attentions with anyone – with the exception of a friend, Wendy MacDonald. Wendy also completed a degree in Scots law, and had secured a diploma with a legal practice in Edinburgh. She told Olivia the company was looking to engage a second trainee and that she'd put in a good word for her.

'You're almost certain to get it, Olivia,' Wendy had told her when she'd phoned a fortnight after leaving St Andrews. 'You should easily find digs in town, and put that creep out of your mind. He can't bother you when he doesn't know where you are. Anyway, I hear on the grapevine he graduated. Apparently he's taken a position with a pharmaceutical company in Fife.'

Unfortunately, her moving to the city hadn't been the end of it.

One evening a couple of weeks after taking up her appointment with Fairbairn and Millar, she and Wendy finished for the day and went for a coffee in nearby Broughton Street. They'd said goodbye afterwards, Wendy boarding a bus for her flat in Goldenacre.

Olivia had crossed the road to await a number 8 bus. A moment or two later, however, she was aware of a dark-blue Toyota RAV4 passing the bus stop. The car slowed to walking speed, and Olivia glanced up and immediately felt her skin crawl. Grossman gave a smile of satisfaction as he saw her mortified look, and drove off.

Olivia had been unable shake off a feeling of dread for the rest of the evening, and hardly slept that night.

After that, she'd avoided taking the number 8, walking instead to Leith Street, where she boarded one of several buses which passed High Street. But she remained wary, giving every dark-blue RAV4 a look of trepidation.

When the following weeks passed without incident, Olivia reasoned Grossman must have just happened to be in town, and that their paths had crossed by coincidence.

The Thursday before Emma was due to arrive, however, she and Wendy had left the office and were chatting on the pavement outside. It was late night shopping and Wendy told her she was heading to Princes Street. Olivia replied that she was preparing for her sister's arrival, and intended popping into a grocer in High Street. As she finished saying this, Olivia had looked along the street and gasped in alarm.

Wendy had turned to see what she was looking at. 'What's the matter?' she said.

At that moment, a car's engine fired, its headlights came on at full beam, and a dark-blue Toyota roared toward them at speed.

Wendy saw her friend's look of apprehension as the car sped past, and said, 'Clive Grossman?'

Olivia nodded. 'I saw him the day we had coffee in Broughton Street, too,' she replied. 'I just put it down to coincidence.'

'You've seen him since?'

'No.'

'Well, he was parked here in Abercromby Place,' Wendy said. 'So he knows where you work. Where you live, too, most likely.' She put her hand on Olivia's arm. 'Look, you've got to contact the police. This isn't going to cease until you file a complaint.'

Olivia dipped her head in acknowledgement. 'I will, Wendy,' she'd said, 'but not until Emma's been. It's only five days. I don't want anything to spoil her visit.'

'Okay,' Wendy said sternly. 'But he's not going to stop until you do something. Promise me you'll take care of it then?'

'I promise,' she'd said.

Olivia was brought back to the present by the sound of a car, which snapped her out of her reverie. She heard a

door slam, footsteps, then a key being turned in the
bedroom door. Grossman entered and crossed the room,
placed a small black bag on the dresser, then swung
around and glanced in her direction.

'Ah, you're awake, Olivia, darling,' he said pleasantly.
'How are you feeling?'

Chapter Five

'Leckie was quick enough to declare his innocence,' Fulton
said as he and Knox drove through Corstorphine on their
way back to Gayfield Square. 'You believe him?'

'Regarding the whereabouts of the jewels, you mean?'
Knox replied.

Fulton nodded. 'Aye.'

Knox slowed for pedestrian crossing lights, which had
just changed to amber.

'Well, the Qatari's diamonds are still unaccounted for,'
he replied. 'Back in 2003 I asked his agent to describe the
box and contents. I remember him telling me it was about
the size of a large box of chocolates. An inch deep, around
a foot long and eight inches in width. Hinged, with a tiny
locking mechanism.'

'Easy to hide,' Fulton said.

'And very valuable,' Knox replied. 'I recall him saying the contents were the most precious of small stones. Clear, flawless, double cut, and around 0.20 carat. He explained that colour affected value. These had been graded "D" and were worth seven hundred dollars each.'

'How many?' Fulton asked.

'Around 2,500,' Knox said. 'Valued at one and three-quarter million dollars back in 2003. Likely to be more now.'

Fulton gave a low whistle. 'Getting on for a couple of million quid?'

'Something like that.'

'Mm-hmm,' Fulton said. 'Leckie said the proceeds of the robbery were stashed at his place, and he never saw the Qatari guy's jewels. Maybe he's right. Any one of the others could have concealed a package like that.'

'I agree,' Knox said.

Fulton thought for a moment. 'Any chance the Arab might have put out a contract?'

Knox shook his head. 'No. The Qatari will have been insured; the loss written off.' Knox paused and added, 'I'm convinced the shooter's nearer home.'

'Charlie O'Dowd, Tommy Salter or Norman McVey?' Fulton asked.

'Highly likely,' Knox replied. 'If one of them is convinced Leckie has the diamonds.'

'But why murder the card players?' Fulton said.

'A cold-blooded act, I agree,' Knox said. 'And I've had another think about the shooter's intentions. I'm getting the feeling it might have been designed as an example – to put the wind up Leckie and make him reveal where the diamonds are.'

'So, what's the next step?' Fulton asked.

The lights turned green and Knox selected first gear and started to move off. 'See if the post-mortem and forensics turn up anything,' Knox replied. 'After that we'll have a word with the other George Street raiders.'

* * *

When McCann and Hathaway exited her car in Abercromby Place, a female traffic warden hastened to the parking bay. 'You can't leave it there,' she said haughtily. 'The ticket machine is out of service. She took a pen from her ticket book and used it as a pointer. 'If you continue along you'll find a space in Heriot Row,' she added, 'the machines there are working.'

McCann flashed her warrant card and nodded to the offices opposite. 'We have an appointment to keep here. Police business.'

'Oh, I see,' the woman said with a disconcerted look. 'That's different then – you can go ahead.'

McCann gave her a derisive nod. 'Thank you.'

The detectives crossed the street, ascended a short flight of steps, and entered the offices of Fairbairn and Millar.

A middle-aged woman looked up as they approached the reception desk and smiled. 'May I help you?' she said.

'We've called to see one of your staff,' McCann said. 'A Ms Wendy MacDonald?'

The woman glanced at her notepad. 'Ah, yes,' she said. 'You're the police officer who phoned a short while ago. You spoke to Ms Breadlove?'

'Yes,' McCann replied.

'Okay.' The receptionist pointed to a door a short distance away. 'Ms Breadlove instructed me to let you have the use of that room. Just go in and take a seat. I'll let Wendy know you're here.'

McCann and Hathaway did so, and a few moments later were joined by a red-headed girl in her early twenties.

'Ms Breadlove said you wanted to see me?' she said, eyeing the officers with a degree of trepidation.

'You're Wendy MacDonald?' McCann asked.

'Yes,' she replied hesitantly.

McCann smiled, then gestured to a chair and said, 'Please, sit down.'

The young woman complied and McCann added, 'We understand you're a friend of Olivia Ledbetter, a law trainee who works with you?'

MacDonald paled. 'Oh, my God, nothing's happened to her, has it?'

McCann ignored the question. 'Olivia's parents have reported her missing. She was last seen on Friday, 14 April when she accompanied her sister to the airport. Olivia failed to return to her flat in Jeffrey Street and isn't answering her mobile.' A pause. 'Her flatmate, Fiona Douglas, tells us you phoned her a little after 4pm yesterday?'

MacDonald nodded. 'Yes. I rang Olivia's mobile on Saturday to ask if she wanted to go for a drink, but got no answer. I tried phoning again on Sunday and her mobile was still switched off. It's not like Olivia, and I was anxious. That's why I called her flat.'

'Ms Douglas tells us you mentioned someone by the name of Grossman?'

'Yes, Clive Grossman.'

'You rang off when Ms Douglas asked who Grossman was?' Hathaway said.

MacDonald gave a little shrug. 'Olivia shares the flat with Ms Douglas,' she said. 'I realised I might be betraying a confidence if I said more.'

'I see,' McCann said. 'What can you tell us about Grossman?'

'Olivia dated him a couple of times while we were at university,' MacDonald replied. 'Made a nuisance of himself when she refused to go out with him again.'

'Olivia told you this?'

'Eventually, yes.'

'Eventually?'

'Yes,' MacDonald replied. 'We only got to know each other in our second year, and became friends soon afterwards. I think it was only then Olivia decided she could confide in me. She told me he was giving her trouble.'

'What kind of trouble?' McCann asked.

MacDonald told them about the phone calls and stalking that had taken place while Olivia had been at St Andrews, and the unwanted gifts she'd received.

'You say she received the parcels just before she came to Edinburgh. Did she see or hear from him again once she arrived?'

MacDonald gave an emphatic nod. 'Yes,' she replied. 'A fortnight after she started here, she saw him while waiting for a bus in Broughton Street. He passed her driving a dark-blue Toyota RAV4. She told me he slowed almost to walking pace until she spotted him, then gave a sort of smirk and drove on.'

'I see, McCann said. 'And when was the last time you saw Olivia?

'A week past Friday when we finished work,' MacDonald said.

'Did she seem okay?' McCann asked. 'After the incident the previous day? She wasn't worried she might run into Grossman again?'

'No, she was in good spirits. Looking forward to spending time with her sister.'

'And you didn't see her or speak to her on the phone the following weekend or at any time in the last week?'

'No,' MacDonald said. 'That Friday was the last time we spoke.'

Chapter Six

'So, two cases, both serious,' Knox was saying. He and his team were gathered in the Major Incident Inquiry Room at Gayfield Square Police Station. The greater part of the open-plan office was taken up by the detectives' workstations. A small briefing area was located at the centre, and the DCI's office, utility rooms and toilets were situated at the opposite end.

A large whiteboard was positioned near a window in the briefing area, where a marker had been used to divide its surface into two sections: the left, headed "Ledbetter/possible abduction"; the right, titled "Triple homicide/Leckie".

'Okay,' Knox went on, 'we'll continue as we are with regard to assignments: Arlene and Mark on the Ledbetter case, myself and Bill on the Spylaw Road shootings. I want the four of us, however, to be *au fait* with both investigations, and I encourage – indeed, expect – a crossover of ideas, hunches and suggestions.'

Knox took a pointer and tapped the left side of the whiteboard, on the corner of which an eight-by-ten-inch photo of the missing girl had been Blu-Tacked. 'Okay,' he continued, 'Olivia Ledbetter, age twenty-one, approximately five foot three inches in height.

'Boarded the last tram into the city centre on Friday, 14 April, arriving in Princes Street at 11.20pm, when she alights. CCTV shows her walking past the RSA Gallery, Scott Monument, turning onto Waverley Bridge, where we lose sight of her. CCTV at a premises near the Market Street junction fails to pick her up within the next ten minutes. Any ideas?'

Hathaway nodded to the whiteboard. 'It's exactly as you've described, boss,' he said. 'Abduction. I'm sure Grossman was waiting for her in his Toyota.'

'Yes, that would certainly fit, given everything Wendy MacDonald told you and Arlene,' Knox said. 'One thing, though: the area's busy, even at 11.30pm on Friday nights. A mainline train station, not to mention bars and restaurants. Which begs the question: how did he get her into his car?'

'He had help?' Hathaway ventured.

'Okay,' Knox said. 'A couple of guys exit a vehicle next to a pavement thronged with pedestrians. Would Olivia really have allowed herself to be taken without screaming the house down? Yet we've heard nothing from the public. Why?'

Hathway shrugged. 'Beats me, boss.'

'I'm not saying it isn't feasible,' Knox said. 'In fact, I think it's highly likely. I just can't see how it could be done without Olivia creating a fuss.'

'What about CCTV at Market Street,' McCann said. 'No sightings of the car?'

Knox shook his head. 'Mark checked the computer as soon as he got back.'

'Sorry, Arlene,' Hathaway said, glancing at McCann. 'I forgot to say. And I had another look at the Princes Street tapes, too; no sign of a RAV4 on those either.' He paused and continued, 'Grossman might have used another vehicle, of course. Even so, the boss is right. Can't see her being taken without protest.'

McCann acknowledged this with a nod and addressed Knox. 'What if Grossman has access to drugs?' She tapped her notebook. 'He graduated as a chemist, works with a pharmaceutical firm in Fife.'

'You mean overpowered her with chloroform or something?' Fulton said. 'Couldn't be done without attracting attention.'

'No… wait,' Knox said, and turned to McCann. 'You're right, Arlene, that's possible. Only there's a chance it happened further back, before she reached Princes Street.'

'On the tram, you mean?' Fulton said.

'Aye,' Knox said, then addressed Hathaway. 'Mark, study the onboard tape after the briefing, will you? Check if anyone approaches her at any point on the journey.'

'Boss,' Hathaway said.

Knox turned his attention to the opposite side of the whiteboard. 'Right, the triple shootings at Spylaw Road. We're still waiting on forensics and the results of the PMs, but my initial hunch is that the murders are linked to the George Street safe-deposit robbery in 2003.'

'I went over your notes, boss,' McCann said. 'You really think Leckie was the reason for the shooter's visit to Spylaw Road?'

Knox nodded. 'I do,' he said. 'As you'll have read, the proceeds of the raid were stashed at his place and shared among the perpetrators afterwards. Around eighty per cent of the haul was recovered, worth four million pounds.'

'Andy O'Dowd gave up his accomplices?' Hathaway asked.

'Yes, he made a deal, served seven months,' Knox replied. 'Out of the picture now, as he's recently deceased. The others were sentenced to terms averaging ten years.'

'A box of diamonds is missing?' McCann asked. 'Valued at 1.75 million dollars. You reckon Leckie planked it?'

Knox dipped his head in affirmation. 'Appears so.'

'What about the card players?' McCann said. 'I had a quick look at their HOLMES records. All three have form. Nothing significant, but still…'

'Were they *all* targets, you mean?' Knox said.

'Yes,' McCann replied.

'We can't discount anything, of course,' Knox replied. 'But I'm of the opinion that the shooter knew that Leckie played every Monday, that he'd be at the game. My hunch is his men were intended to be sacrificial lambs.'

'To drive home the point that the killer meant business?' Hathaway said.

'Yes,' Knox said. 'Callous, I'll grant you. But, as I say, the idea was to make Leckie talk.'

Knox checked his watch. 'Okay,' he said. 'We'll get the ball rolling after lunch.' He nodded towards Hathaway and said, 'Mark, after you check the tram, give St Andrews University a ring. I want everything they have on Grossman: date of birth, home address, parents' details, et cetera.'

Then to McCann he said, 'Arlene, get in touch with the pharmaceutical company in Fife. We need employment details, and whether or not Grossman has access to drugs. Cross-check addresses with anything Mark uncovers.'

Knox thumbed towards the workstations and finally addressed Fulton, 'Bill, find out the current addresses of O'Dowd, Salter and McVey. If they're reasonably local, we'll see them this afternoon. He nodded to the DCI's office. 'I'm going to bring Warburton up to date.'

* * *

'Not speaking, Olivia dear?' Grossman was saying. 'Still a little groggy?'

Grossman took the ladder-backed chair, placed it next to the bed and sat down.

Olivia glared at him. 'Don't come near me,' she warned.

Grossman gave a supercilious smile. 'Don't be concerned, darling,' he said. 'I put you to bed, but had no intention of taking advantage.'

'Then why have you brought me here?' A pause. 'And where *is* here?'

'Why?' Grossman said. 'I thought that would have been obvious, darling. You received all my notes, didn't you? You know how much I love you.'

Olivia gave him a look of incredulity. 'Surely you're not serious.' she said. 'I made it plain I didn't want to see you again.'

'You didn't feel that way to begin with,' Grossman replied, feigning hurt. 'You were attracted to me then.'

'That's simply not true,' Olivia replied, shaking her head in frustration. 'Clive, you have to stop this. Are you aware of what you're doing? You have to let me go. I promise I won't bring charges.'

'Of course I'm aware,' Grossman said. 'And before long you won't feel like bringing charges, since you'll be so used to us being together.'

'You don't understand,' Olivia protested, 'this is *abduction*. My mother and father were to have called me last night. They'll have realised something's wrong by now and contacted the police. You'll be in trouble when they find me.'

'But that's the point, darling: they just *won't* find you. You asked where you were? Well, let's just say it's an exceptionally remote area. You're presently in a cottage set in fifty acres of private land, no main roads within miles.

'You remember me telling you about my aunt?' he continued. 'Well, she passed a little over a year ago, and left me a considerable sum. It enabled me to buy this property soon after we met. I intended it as a surprise after I proposed. But we never got that far, did we?'

Olivia shook her head in exasperation. 'Look, Clive, I'll say it again – I don't have any feelings for you. We met twice in a kind of friendship. Two people in a new environment spending time together – that's all there was to it.'

Grossman gave her a patronising smile. 'Really?' he said. 'If you'll pardon me, darling, I think you'll feel differently before long. And there's a valid reason why.' He paused. 'You've heard of arranged marriages? Very common in some countries. India and Pakistan, of course, but did you know it's practised in other parts of Asia, too, like China and Japan?

'Couples from different towns and villages, betrothed by their parents, complete strangers on their wedding day. Why should it be different in the West? Are all those couples in love when they meet? Of course not. Yet they become closer in time. Which is how it'll be with us. Except that the honeymoon period will come first. Marriage can wait until you learn to love me.'

Olivia was seriously beginning to doubt Grossman's sanity. 'You really mean it?' she said. 'You intend keeping me here against my will?'

'Only until you come round to my way of thinking, darling,' he said, and waved at their surroundings. 'You'll stay in this room for a week or two, until you get used to the idea. The door has a double mortice and the window is similarly secure, so you won't feel tempted to try anything when I'm out. Incidentally, I've taken a note of your sizes and will make sure you've an adequate change of clothing.

'I'll cook and bring your meals to you, too, of course, as I'll be here most of the time now I've left my position with G&R Pharmaceuticals.' He pointed to a cupboard on the left of the television. 'Oh, and I've arranged for your, ahem, other needs if I don't happen to be here. There's a chemical toilet in that closet.'

Olivia's anger subsided, replaced by a growing sense of despair. On the positive side, she realised her parents would have tried to call her. They'd have been in touch with Fiona Douglas, too, and would have come to the conclusion that something was wrong.

But there was also the negative: she was in no doubt that Grossman had a warped sense of reality. The clinical planning of her abduction and the manner in which it was executed – injecting her with a strong sedative – demonstrated that he was dangerous.

'My iPhone,' she said, forcing herself to sound calm. 'What did you do with it?'

'I'm sorry, Olivia,' Grossman replied. 'I had to get rid of it. I didn't want to run the risk of it pinpointing your location. I switched it off, removed the sim card, and disposed of both. Don't worry, darling, I promise to replace it at some point.'

Olivia couldn't help herself, but a well of despondency suddenly rose, and she found herself sobbing uncontrollably.

Grossman fetched a box of tissues from the dressing table and placed them on the bed beside her. 'Don't cry, darling,' he said and motioned towards the bedroom door. 'There's a bathroom and shower next door, and the water's hot. You'll find a change of underthings and a dressing gown, and afterwards I'll bring you a nice cup of tea.' He took a tissue from the box and proffered it to her. 'We'll soon have you feeling better.'

Chapter Seven

Fulton's search of computer records unearthed the present locations of three of the four men who carried out the George Street security deposit raid. Charlie O'Dowd, the gang's leader, now aged fifty-six, was living at a bungalow in the Priestfield area of Edinburgh. Thomas Salter, now fifty-three, who at the time of the robbery stayed in Manderston Street in Leith, now resided in Redford Way, one of a series of new housing developments which had sprung up on the periphery of the city. Norman McVey was the only one of the gang who still lived at the same address – 245 Harbour Terrace, Prestonpans. And it was he whom Knox decided to interview first.

The afternoon was sunny and warm, and Knox and Fulton decided to take the coast road, driving parallel to the Firth of Forth via Joppa and Musselburgh.

'You don't think we should have given him a bell?' Fulton said. 'Made sure he was home?'

Knox shook his head. 'Element of surprise, Bill. Always the best policy with felons.'

Fulton grinned. 'Take them off guard, eh, boss?' he said. 'Don't give them time to fabricate a story?'

'Exactly,' Knox replied. 'Of course if he isn't home we'll have had a bit of a wasted journey, but hey…'

'Not a bad day for a run down the coast?'

'Aye, not bad at all,' Knox agreed.

The detectives fell silent for several moments, then Fulton said, 'McVey was the oldest of the bunch – forty-three at the time of the raid. He'll be in his early sixties now.'

'Clean sheet since 2003?' Knox asked.

Fulton nodded. 'Aye, him and O'Dowd. Salter did another spell in Saughton between 2015 and 2017. Breaking and entering – a warehouse in Leith.'

'Anything else since his release?'

'Who, McVey?'

'Yes.'

Fulton took out his iPhone. 'I'll check,' he said. 'I downloaded the files before I left the station.' He scrolled through the iPhone's screen, found the file he was looking for, and studied the document for a moment or two. 'No,' he continued, 'McVey got out in 2011, reported to his parole officer until late 2014, was given a full release and has kept his nose clean since.

'A social service update added to his file in 2013 states he was seriously injured at work – Granston's Wire Mill in Musselburgh – when a forklift backed into him. Wheelchair bound now, the accident cost him the use of his legs.'

'Hh-mm,' Knox said. 'Strong basis for him not being the shooter.'

Fulton checked the document again. 'The social service addendum is on the foot of page three of the desktop file, boss. Sorry, I never spotted it. Might have saved us the journey if I had.'

'No, Bill, that's okay. No harm in interviewing him. Might prove useful.'

As Knox spoke they entered Prestonpans, where his sat nav directed him to 245 Harbour Terrace, the end house in a row of former miner's cottages.

When the detectives exited the car a young man in motorbike leathers appeared from the corner of the house and stared at them. 'Looking for someone?' he asked.

'Yes,' Knox replied. 'Mr Norman McVey. You know him?'

The man was fair-haired, athletic-looking and appeared to be in his late twenties. 'My dad,' he said, thumbing over his shoulder. 'In the back, tending the garden.' He studied Knox for a moment. 'And you are?'

Knox showed him his warrant card. 'Detective Inspector Knox and Detective Sergeant Fulton.'

'Right,' he replied. 'Follow me and I'll take you to him.'

The detectives did as they were asked and arrived at the rear of the cottage, where a man in a wheelchair was clipping an outgrowth of leaves at a hedge beside a low wall.

'Dad!' their escort called out. 'Two men to see you. Police.'

Norman McVey turned, gave the detectives a brief nod, then used a pair of secateurs to wave in the direction of a garden bench. 'Take a seat, lads,' he said. 'Just cutting back on this hawthorn bush. Be with you in a sec.'

The detectives complied and a minute later McVey put down the secateurs, steered the wheelchair in their direction, and stopped opposite the seat. 'So, lads,' he said. 'To what do I owe the pleasure?'

'You're Norman McVey?' Knox asked.

'Yes.'

'I'm DI Knox and this is DS Fulton. We're here to ask if you can assist us with an inquiry. It concerns–'

At that moment, his son interrupted. 'Dad,' he said. 'I'm away in to get changed and take a shower.'

'Aye, right, Ron,' McVey said. 'Tell your ma I'll be in directly.'

His son gave a brief nod, turned, and went back the way he had come.

'Ronnie's a keen biker,' McVey said, gesturing to a shed in the corner of the garden. 'He was putting his machine away just before you arrived. Wee bit of a conflict with his fiancée, Lorna, though; the girl can't abide motorbikes.' McVey gave a little laugh. 'I can see him having to get rid of it when they're married.' He noted the detectives' bland expressions. 'Sorry, I'm blethering; you mentioned something about an inquiry?'

'Yes,' Knox said. 'As I was about to say, it concerns Hugh Leckie.'

'Shug?' McVey said curiously. 'What's up with him?'

'Three of his employees were murdered yesterday at a property he owns in Spylaw Road, Edinburgh. Mr Leckie was to have been there, but was called away due to his mother being ill.' Knox paused. 'We were wondering if you'd heard anything?'

'Really?' McVey shook his head. 'That's bad… No, sorry, I haven't seen Shug in years.'

'When was the last time you saw him?' Knox asked.

'Got to be a while,' McVey said. He stroked his chin and was silent for a few moments. 'Let's see, I ran into him in the high street a couple of years after I was released from Saughton. That'd be around 2013. We went to The Mitre for a pint, had a bit of a chinwag. I recall him saying he was getting into the property business and asking if I was interested in working for him. I told him thanks but no thanks, I'd just started as a storeman with Granston's, and was happy with the job. He said if I changed my mind to get in touch. But I never did.'

McVey nodded to the house, where the outline of woman at a sink was visible through the translucent glass of a window. 'After I did my time, I promised Ella I'd avoid the crowd I mucked around with then and go straight. It's a promise I've kept.'

'So 2013 was the last time you saw him?' Fulton asked.

'Aye,' McVey said. 'I told you, in The Mitre.'

'And before that?' Knox said.

'Would have been at the share-out after the George Street job,' McVey said.

'In the presence of the others involved – Charlie and Andy O'Dowd, and Thomas Salter?' Knox asked.

'Aye, likely.'

'Do you recall the matter of a box of diamonds being discussed?'

McVey leaned back in the wheelchair, smiled, and shook his head. 'The Arab's jewels?' he said. 'Only after it was reported in the papers. I assure you, Inspector...' He paused and gave Knox a querying look, clearly having forgotten his name.

'Detective Inspector Knox,' Knox said.

'Aye, Detective Inspector Knox,' McVey said. 'I assure you that none of us saw any diamonds. The Arab must have been telling porkies – for the insurance.'

Knox dipped his head in acknowledgement. 'How well do you know Leckie?' he asked.

McVey shrugged his shoulders. 'Well, like I say, I haven't seen him in ages.'

'At the time, I mean,' Knox said.

'Back then?' McVey said. 'I dunno, we were good pals, I suppose. If I was down on my luck, he'd slip me a few quid. And, naturally, I'd do the same for him.' He nodded to the window again. 'Back in 2001, Ella was in a bad way. Took a sudden bleeding of the uterus; had to have a hysterectomy. She was at her wit's end, as I was inside, doing time for a break-in. She phoned Shug's wife Joan – since passed, God bless her. Joan and Shug looked after Ronnie while Ella was in hospital.

'Shug and I met up again after I got out, of course. Did a few jobs, either separately or together, after which either he or I would get huckled.' McVey sighed audibly. 'Pretty much how it was till the CincScot Security job. As I've said, we went our separate ways after that.'

'Okay,' Knox said. 'One final question, Mr McVey. Might seem a bit unnecessary, but I've still got to ask it. Where were you yesterday evening?'

McVey gave Knox an impassive look. 'It's okay, I know the drill.' He tapped one side of his wheelchair. 'Where I usually am at that time most days, Inspector. Parked in an armchair in front of the fire, reading a book. Bugger all on telly worth watching.'

* * *

Olivia felt better after she'd showered and changed. She put on the plain white dressing gown Grossman had left, which was a perfect fit, but experienced a shiver of revulsion when she examined the briefs and found they too were the correct size.

As promised, a cup of tea was waiting on her return, and at 1pm Grossman brought in a small table, on which he'd placed a tray with her lunch. He did the same at 6pm, giving her a choice between haddock and chips or roast beef and potatoes.

He said little on either occasion. At lunchtime he gestured to the television after placing a remote on the bedside table. 'The TV's permanently tuned to a movie channel, Olivia,' he said. 'So I'm afraid you'll be unable to do anything except adjust the volume or switch it off. I've arranged it that way as I'd rather you didn't watch any news channels. I don't want you upset by coverage of your disappearance.'

He said nothing more until he cleared away the dishes after dinner, when he indicated the bedroom door. 'It'll be locked only when I'm out of the house,' he explained. 'As you're aware, the shower and toilet are next door, which you can continue to use. To the left and right of the hallway beyond are the front and rear doors – both locked, of course. Further along is the kitchen, living room and my bedroom and study, all of which are off limits for now.' He smiled. 'Any contravention will result in my having to

47

lock you in your bedroom again. You understand, don't you, dear?'

Olivia gave a cursory nod in reply.

'Good,' Grossman said. 'Then I'll wish you goodnight. Oh, by the way, I've installed a buzzer next to the bedside table in case you need me. Only for emergencies, though – yes?'

She lay in bed afterwards and watched a few minutes of a romantic comedy, then switched the TV off and went to the window, outside of which a wire grill had been fitted. Daylight was beginning to fade as she opened the blinds and saw a wide stretch of pasture, and beyond that a thick row of birch trees. The setting sun glinted off water behind the treeline, suggesting a stream.

She turned her attention to the opposite end of the room, where an area at the left corner had been curtained off. The curtain – an orange damask material – was suspended from a rail at the ceiling.

Olivia drew it back to reveal a small alcove illuminated by a narrow sash window. The bottom half had been glazed with frosted glass, but the upper pane was transparent. Olivia entered and looked out.

Grossman hadn't been exaggerating when he'd spoken about the property's acreage. The ground at the rear of the cottage sloped gently to a broad meadow, at the far side of which were more trees; a medium-sized wood of oak, willow and elder nestling beneath a series of rolling hills.

Olivia's attention was drawn to the window sash, which had been rendered immovable by a pair of aluminium L-brackets fixed at either side.

Clearly it would be impossible to escape that way.

She remembered that Grossman had mentioned a gated track, which meant a proper road must be near. And where there was a road, she reasoned, there would also be cars.

The trees lining the stream appeared to head in that direction. All she had to do was reach cover and make a run for it.

But that would mean gaining Grossman's confidence.

If she could persuade him she was becoming amenable, it was possible he'd allow her outside, even if he insisted on acting as chaperone.

She was convinced that in such a scenario he'd only have to let his guard down once…

Chapter Eight

'No corroboration for McVey, boss,' Fulton was saying, 'since he's only got his missus to vouch for him. But I'd say his alibi's watertight.'

The detectives were heading back towards town, Knox having forsaken the coast road in favour of the A1 bypass.

'I agree, Bill, no question,' Knox said.

The brake lights of the vehicles ahead came on as he spoke and Knox took his foot off the accelerator and tapped the brake pedal. Seconds later, he'd dropped into second gear and was soon moving at less than twenty miles per hour.

Fulton shifted in his seat, craning his neck to get a better view. 'Old Craighall Interchange up ahead,' he said. 'Looks like an RTA.'

Knox glanced at his watch. 'Almost 4.30pm. I was hoping to drop in on Charlie O'Dowd on the way back. Looks like I may have to put it off until tomorrow.'

Fulton nodded. 'Yeah, at least he and Salter stay in the city.'

The vehicles in both lanes were now moving at walking pace. Knox took out his iPhone, placed it on the dash bracket, and switched to speakers. 'I promised to give Turley a ring,' he said. 'He should have finished the PMs by now.'

Knox scrolled through the address book, found Turley's number, and moments later the call connected.

'Turley,' the pathologist replied.

'Alex?' Knox said. 'Jack Knox. Said I'd give you a ring.'

'Right, Jack,' Turley replied. 'Aye, all three PMs have been done. Found the other two slugs and passed them on to ballistics. Similar head trauma in all three cases. Nothing else, except to say that the gunman knew his stuff. The body positions of Scott and Reilly indicate they had little time to react. Hit a fraction of a second after he came into the room. That's a fair degree of accuracy.'

'Noted, Alex,' Knox said. 'And thanks.'

'No problem, Jack,' Turley said. 'Oh, by the way, I got a call from Lucy Carmichael around an hour ago.'

'Oh, yes?'

'Aye, she'll be back next Monday. Can't say I'm not looking forward to her return. Didn't realise how much I'd been enjoying retirement.'

Knox laughed. 'I find that hard to believe, Alex.'

'Which?' Turley replied. 'Looking forward to her return, or enjoying my retirement?' He paused. 'It's okay, Jack, don't answer that. Though we know what the answer would be in your case.'

'Now, now, Alex,' Knox said. 'You're misbehaving again.'

'Don't mean to tell me you haven't heard from her lately?' Turley said.

'I told you this morning, Alex, we're not as close as you'd like to believe.'

'Aye, right,' Turley said. 'Okay, Jack, take care.'

'You too, Alex. Bye.'

Knox ended the call and turned to see Fulton grinning. 'What?' he said.

'Never said a word, boss,' Fulton replied.

At that moment, Knox's phone lit up and the ringtone began to reverberate through the speakers.

Knox tapped *accept* and a voice said, 'Jack? Ed Murray. Just received the initial reports on Spylaw Road.'

'Okay, Ed,' Knox said. 'Carry on.'

'We managed to isolate prints from the gunman's footwear from those of the others,' Murray said. 'They've a unique pattern, but so far we've not managed to track down the manufacturer. We're continuing to check. As soon as we get a result I'll let you know.'

'What about fingerprints?'

'On the BT bill? No, sorry, Jack, he doesn't appear to have touched it.'

'And DNA?' Knox asked.

'Yes,' Murray said. 'I was coming to that. We found a single hair on the leg of the chair the gunman kicked. Most likely transferred from the shoes or boots he wore. We're currently examining the root fibre to see if we can extract anything.'

'But it's not guaranteed?' Knox said.

'Afraid not.'

'How long will it take?'

'We're hoping a couple of days,' Murray replied. 'Sometimes it takes longer.'

'You'll let me know if you're successful?'

'Soon as, Jack.'

'Okay, Ed,' Knox said. 'Thanks.'

* * *

Knox and Fulton arrived back in the office at 5.40pm, after a delay – due to a pile-up of a jack-knifed trailer and three cars – of forty-five minutes. McCann and Hathaway were still at their desks, and brought Knox up to date on the results of their inquiries into Olivia Ledbetter's disappearance.

'St Andrews gave us Clive Grossman's home address,' McCann said. '41 Prideaux Terrace, Padstow, Cornwall. We contacted Devon and Cornwall Police and an Inspector Davis got back to us about an hour ago.'

'And?'

'He tells us the place was a fairly substantial manor house, set in its own grounds.'

'Was?' Knox said.

'Yes,' McCann replied. 'Mrs Gosling, nee Grossman – Clive's aunt – died a year and a half ago. Clive Grossman inherited the property and her estate. He sold it to a real estate developer four months later. Davis told me Mrs Gosling had been acting in loco parentis since Clive's parents divorced fifteen years ago. His father was an alcoholic, apparently. His mother remarried. To an American – now lives in Florida.'

'Clive Grossman,' Knox said. 'Has he any form?'

'Got into a bit of trouble when he was eleven,' McCann replied. 'Caught shoplifting at a local chemist's. Passed on to a local magistrate, after which the owner decided not to press charges.'

McCann tapped an A4 sheet on her desk. 'Another snippet of info I found interesting. Davis unearthed a report from a child psychiatrist which was passed on to the magistrate when he was deliberating the case. The shrink described Grossman as, "generally withdrawn, some evidence of OCD. The child has impulsive thoughts and images which can cause intense anxiety. A course of selective serotonin reuptake inhibitors recommended."'

'*Very* interesting,' Knox agreed. 'What about St Andrews?'

'Did they report anything unusual, you mean?' McCann asked.

'Yes.'

McCann shook her head. 'No. Model student, graduated in November last year with a degree in chemistry. St Andrews says he got a start with a company called G&R Pharmaceuticals at Donibristle in Fife in January this year.' McCann turned to Hathaway. 'Mark's been in touch and can tell you more – Mark?'

'Yeah, boss,' Hathaway said, addressing Knox. 'G&R's manager told me Grossman started on 9 January, splitting his duties between the company's lab research department and their wholesale warehouse, which dispenses drugs to chemists and hospitals. The manager, a Mr Colin Medwin, told me when Grossman wasn't engaged in lab work he acted as an assistant in charge of fulfilling drug orders, many of them listed under the DDA heading.'

'DDA?' Fulton said.

'Yeah,' Hathaway said. 'Dangerous Drugs Act; all require a signature on collection or delivery.'

'Okay,' Knox said. 'Go on.'

'Grossman gave a week's notice and finished up on 31 March. Mr Medwin tells me the following week a stocktaking was undertaken in the DDA department, and certain drugs were found to be missing.'

'Which drugs?' Knox asked.

'Ten ampules of 1mg ketamine,' Hathaway said. 'And a 50mg bottle of pentobarbital. Grossman was responsible for storage and administration of the drugs together with four others. Mr Medwin is anxious to speak to him with regard to their disappearance.'

'G&R thinks he might have taken them?' Knox asked.

'That's just it,' Hathaway said. 'Medwin emphasised that at the moment the company is reluctant to apportion blame. They're currently doing a thorough search of the department, and speaking to employees.'

'Did you ask Medwin what the drugs were used for?'

Hathaway nodded. 'Yes, ketamine is a fast-acting anaesthetic, used by doctors to sedate patients.'

'And pentobarbital?'

'Medwin told me the company mostly exports it to clinics in Switzerland, where it's used for euthanasia.'

'Jesus,' Fulton said. 'So it's likely Grossman nicked these before he terminated his employment?'

'Medwin is not saying as much,' Hathaway said. 'Only that the company would like to speak to him.'

'They tried the address he gave?' Knox asked.

'Yes,' Hathaway replied. 'They sent one of their managers to the address listed when he joined the company – 16 Forth Street, St Andrews, which was where he stayed as a student. But he moved out late last year, leaving no forwarding address.'

'What about a phone?' Fulton asked.

'Yeah, he gave a mobile number,' Hathaway replied. 'Medwin tells me he's tried ringing several times, but received no answer.'

Knox pursed his lips. 'Looks like it's beginning to fall into place: Olivia *was* drugged. That's how Grossman was able to abduct her.' He paused and nodded to Hathaway's desktop. 'You've looked at the Lothian Transport tram tapes?'

'I'd just started when you came back to the office, boss,' Hathaway said. He clicked a mouse on his desktop computer, and an image of a tram's interior filled the screen.

The detectives crowded around the desktop as Hathaway indicated a counter at the top right. 'The tram leaves the airport at twelve minutes to eleven,' he said. 'I'm at 22.45, when Olivia enters the carriage – see, she sits immediately forward of the luggage rack.'

McCann dipped her head towards the screen. 'Exactly what her sister told her parents she was wearing,' she said. 'Three-quarter length navy-blue parka, orange bobble hat, pale-blue jeans, grey and white Adidas trainers.'

Hathaway clicked on the top left corner and the view changed. 'This gives us a shot of the remainder of the carriage,' he said. 'As you can see, it's quiet. A couple seated two rows ahead of her, a middle-aged couple at the other side. Other than that, it's empty.'

Knox tapped the top left corner. 'Let's see the other view again. Roll it until the tram starts moving.'

As Hathaway did so, the image reverted to a view of Olivia seated in front of a luggage section. He clicked again, and the counter moved first to 22.46, then 22.47.

At 22.48, a few moments before the carriage doors closed, a man boarded and took one of a row of seats facing the luggage rack. He wore a grey three-quarter-length jacket with a hood pulled over his head. He also wore a black face mask and carried a small backpack, which he removed and placed on the seat beside him.

Knox pointed to the screen. 'There's our man,' he said.

'Olivia glanced at him as he sat down,' Fulton said. 'She doesn't appear to recognise him.'

'Of course not,' McCann said. 'He's too well disguised.'

'How long does it take to reach the city centre?' Knox said to Hathaway.

'Five stops before it reaches Haymarket, boss,' Hathaway replied. 'Around twenty-five minutes.'

Knox nodded. 'Roll forward a bit,' he said. 'I want to see if he's watching her.'

Hathaway clicked on the fast-forward button and the video speeded up. The detectives were watching as the tram arrived and departed the next three stops, when Hathaway pointed to the counter and said, 'Edinburgh Park Station, 23.01. That's the last stop outside the city centre. The next one is Murrayfield, followed by Haymarket.'

'Not aware of him taking an overt interest,' Fulton commented.

'Oh, but he's watching her all right,' McCann said. 'Which is why he took a bench seat, not one facing the direction of travel.'

'I agree,' Knox said. 'And why keep his pack to hand when there's a luggage station opposite?'

'Easier to access?' Fulton said.

Knox gave a confirmative nod. 'How long from where it is now to Haymarket, Mark?'

Hathaway consulted a notebook on his desk. 'Twelve minutes, boss. 23.13.'

'Okay,' Knox said. Continue to fast-forward until just before we reach the stop, around 23.11.'

Hathaway restarted fast forward, returning to normal speed at 23.10. A minute later the detectives saw Grossman reach into the backpack and retrieve a small object.

'What is that?' Knox asked, pointing at the screen.

'Can't make it out,' McCann said.

'Go back, Mark,' Knox said. 'Get ready to freeze-frame when he reaches into the pack.'

Hathaway rewound the video, stopped at 23.09, and played the images forward in slow motion.

'There,' Knox said a few moments later. 'Stop.'

Hathaway complied and all four detectives studied the image closely. 'Looks like a syringe,' McCann said.

'That's exactly what it is,' Knox said. 'Quite the expert, isn't he? It's taken him only a second or two to extract the contents of the ampule.' He paused. 'Okay, Mark, normal speed. I'd bet a tenner he's going to do something and exit at Haymarket.'

Hathaway restarted the video and the detectives saw Grossman palm the needle in his left hand, rise and press the stop bell, then lift his backpack and drop it between the seats where Olivia was sitting. In one swift movement, he reached underneath and injected the syringe into her calf with his left hand, retrieved the backpack with his right, and stood up again.

'She probably wasn't aware what had happened,' McCann said.

The counter at the top right read 23.13 when the carriage door slid open and Grossman exited. Knox pointed to the screen. 'Pound to a penny his car's parked somewhere near,' he said.

Chapter Nine

A Forth Valley consultant told Leckie his mother had suffered a mild stroke, and was likely to be in hospital for five days. For this reason he decided there was no need for him to remain at the Travelodge, as he would drive through from Edinburgh to visit her.

He paid his bill and made his way back to the city, mulling over the day's events. He'd been genuinely shocked by the killings of Tam, Rab and Billy.

DI Knox had implied that other members of the George Street raid were suspected. Leckie gave an involuntary shake of the head, flicked the indicator of his Mercedes GLA at a motorway slip road and joined the M9.

Charlie, Tommy or Norrie the shooter? He found that hard to believe.

In 2003 they'd ransacked the vault of CincScot Security in George Street, each determined to transfer as much loot as possible into heavy-duty garden sacks and get the hell out of there. They'd moved the gear to the back exit at Hill Street South Lane, where a Transit waited with Andy O'Dowd at the wheel.

They drove to his cottage at Gorebridge where the haul was divvied up. It was mostly jewellery, but there'd also been a fair amount of small ingots, Krugerrands, American Gold Eagles, Britannias and cash.

The newspapers had put the value at five million. Subsequent raids on the homes of all five recovered loot worth just under three million. That left a couple of million plus in cash and gold, which – as far as he knew – the others had stashed away in places the bizzies wouldn't find, to be retrieved once they'd served their time.

At least that's what he'd done. Tommy and Charlie, too, judging from the homes they bought within a year of their release. Norrie also appeared to have done well. Leckie heard that he and his missus had taken a Caribbean cruise, and spent at least £20,000 on an extension to their place in Prestonpans.

Which left the wheelman. Andy O'Dowd's share amounted to around £500,000, mostly jewels, which the bizzies seized when he was arrested within days of the raid. Charlie later told him that DCI Fletcher, the officer investigating, had leaned heavily on Andy, threatening a fifteen-year sentence, as opposed to two years or less if he talked. Charlie excused his brother, saying Andy had a three-year-old son. The prospect of not seeing the kid until he was in his teens had been the reason he cracked.

Leckie and the others thought differently: Andy had been unhappy with his cut and hated the prospect of doing hard time. Those were the real reasons he'd given them up. In the event, the younger O'Dowd served only nine months in an open prison, during which time he was attacked on several occasions, as nobody had time for a grass.

Leckie was equally confident no one had witnessed the sleight of hand used to switch the Arab's diamonds from their original safe-deposit box into one he'd rented from CincScot. In the general hubbub in the vault that evening, with four of them noisily prising open safe-deposit doors, he had quietly transferred the diamonds, locked the drawer, and placed the key his pocket.

Even if he had been spotted, he couldn't imagine that justifying the murder of three people – four if Leckie himself was a target.

So if one of the others wasn't the gunman, who was? A hitman working for the Qatari owner? He didn't think so. Why wait till he'd been out of jail for eleven years? That didn't make sense.

Leckie cast his mind back to 2002, two months before his discharge from Saughton. He'd got wind of the job from an old lag called Eddie Robertson, who told him he'd worked out a way to bypass CincScot's alarm system. What's more, Robertson had reliable info that box 535 was worth a fortune, as an Arab billionaire kept it stashed with gemstones he regularly took to Amsterdam to be made into necklaces for mistresses and high-class hookers.

Thing was, Robertson was doing a ten-year stretch at the time and obviously couldn't do the job himself. So he'd said that if Leckie was interested, he'd be happy to take five per cent.

Leckie had been interested. After his release, he'd spent a good three months checking the place, finding weak spots and figuring out the best time to carry out the heist.

He had approached the firm posing as a rich businessman, and when shown the vault, he discovered that box 535 stood at shoulder height. Leckie managed to secure box 518, the row immediately above, which had made the transfer a piece of cake...

Leckie was jolted out of his reverie when he realised he'd taken the wrong traffic lane at Blackhall. Traffic filtering to the right was headed for Ravelston. Leckie's flat was at Ravelston Garden, and he'd moved into the right-hand lane without thinking.

Leckie remembered DI Knox's advice that it might be safer to relocate for a while, as whoever killed Tam, Rab and Billy might still be looking for him.

He changed lanes and continued along Queensferry Road, and ten minutes later turned into Balmoral Place, a cul-de-sac backing onto the Water of Leith.

Number forty-six Balmoral Place was at the end of the street, accessed by an outside flight of stairs. Leckie climbed these, selected a key from a bunch in his pocket, and let himself in.

It was a small furnished house, consisting of a bedroom, kitchen, living room and bathroom. Leckie found that Billy, his late factor, had left a selection of items in the kitchen cupboard, which included tea bags, sugar, and a packet of dehydrated milk.

Leckie brought a kettle to the boil, made a cup of tea, and took it through to the living room. He placed the cup on a coffee table, and sat on an armchair next to a gas fire, which he lit.

Then suddenly his mobile rang. Leckie glanced at the screen and saw it was his office secretary, Kirsty.

'Hi, Kirsty,' he said. 'What's up?'

'I didn't know whether to bother you or not, Mr Leckie,' she said. 'I wasn't sure if you'd still be in Falkirk. Your mother…'

'No, I'm back in Edinburgh,' Leckie said. 'My ma's okay. Slight stroke. Likely she'll be discharged within a week.'

'Oh, glad to hear it's not too bad,' Kirsty replied. 'I hope she recovers soon.'

'So,' Leckie said, 'what's the problem?'

'The Moray Place properties, Mr Leckie. The FRG group. I've had their secretary on the phone twice, asking if you'd completed the paperwork.'

Leckie remembered the deal: two adjacent houses in New Town he'd been in the process of selling to a London outfit, who wanted to convert them to a hotel. They'd agreed a price, and he'd promised to sign the papers and have them couriered south today.

'Sorry, Kirsty, I forgot,' he said. 'Get Frankie to bring them over, will you?'

Frankie was a teenager Leckie employed to shuffle papers around the city on his moped.

'Of course, Mr Leckie,' Kirsty said. 'I'll have him bring them to Ravelston right away.'

'No, Kirsty, I'm not at Ravelston – I'll explain why later. Have him bring them to me at 46, Balmoral Place.'

There was a pause while she wrote down the address. 'Got that, Mr Leckie.'

'Oh and, Kirsty?' Leckie said. 'Get him to bring the contract for the builder's quote for Spylaw Road, while you're at it. May as well get that signed off today, too.'

* * *

Grossman brought a small armchair into the room after breakfast on Sunday. 'The high-backed chair's okay for sitting at the table when taking your meals,' he told Olivia. 'But I think you'll find this a little more comfortable at other times.'

'Thank you,' she said, forcing a smile.

He smiled back. 'Did you enjoy breakfast? Scrambled eggs with bacon is about the best I can do. No good at cooking eggs any other way – I keep bursting the yolks.'

'They were fine,' Olivia replied.

He glanced at her curiously. 'Good,' he replied, and nodded towards the door. 'I have to go out this morning, Olivia,' he said. 'Shops. I'm afraid I'll have to lock the door again.' He glanced at his watch and added, 'Just after ten, now, I should be back in time to make lunch.'

'I understand,' she said.

He gave her a more searching look, registering surprise at her sudden change of mood. 'Is there anything you'd like when I'm out – a magazine, maybe, or a paperback?'

'A magazine, please,' she replied. 'Anything interesting – you choose.'

Grossman smiled again. 'Fine, darling,' he said. 'I'll see what's available.'

He returned just before one o'clock, unlocked the bedroom door, entered and gave her a copy of *Cosmopolitan*. 'Not much variety at the local newsagents,' he said. 'That okay?'

'Yes,' she replied. 'It's one of my favourites.'

The pleasantries continued in a similar vein for the remainder of Sunday and into Monday, when at lunchtime he said, 'I'm having a go at making beef casserole for dinner, Olivia. I thought perhaps instead of having your meal here you'd care to join me in the sitting room?'

'Yes, thank you. That would make a pleasant change.'

At a little after seven, he knocked quietly and popped his head around the door. 'Dinner's almost ready to serve, darling,' he said. 'If you'd care to come along.'

She followed him along the hallway to the opposite end of the cottage, where he waved her into a large room with a bay window. An oak table in the centre of the room had been covered with a lace tablecloth, and two places were set.

Grossman pulled out a chair which Olivia took, then he set down a casserole dish and motioned towards it. 'Please, help yourself.'

After they'd eaten, he rose and took a bottle of wine from a cabinet opposite, placed two glasses on the table, opened the bottle, and poured. 'Cabernet sauvignon,' he said. 'A really nice variety – Napa Valley, California.'

'I wouldn't know,' Olivia said pleasantly. 'I'm not really a wine buff.'

'Really, darling?' Grossman said. 'Oh, I'm sure you'll like this one – it's a bit special.' He indicated the glass. 'Take a swallow, tell me what you think.'

Olivia took a sip and gave a nod of appreciation.

'Good, isn't it?' he said. 'Now, darling, I want you to be completely honest. What did you think of the casserole?'

Olivia's plan to make him think she'd accepted the situation appeared to be working.

'I enjoyed it very much,' she said.

Grossman rolled his shoulders. 'You're not just saying that to be kind?'

'No, it was very nice.'

He studied her for a long moment. 'You know, Olivia, you've changed since Friday,' he said. 'And I've been wondering why.'

'I'm not sure I know what you mean,' Olivia said.

Grossman took another sip of wine. 'The fact that I brought you here against your will,' he said. 'Frankly, I thought it would take longer for you to cooperate. Yet here you are, having dinner and drinking wine with me.'

Olivia shrugged her shoulders. 'You're right,' she said. 'I have changed my mind. I'm aware of the situation and am attempting to make the best of it. You believe I'll come around to your way of thinking, whilst I hope to be able to persuade you to the contrary.' She paused for a moment. 'We're civilised adults, after all. Isn't it better to arrive at a resolution that way than by conflict?'

Grossman laughed. 'Yes, darling, you're right, maybe civility is a better course of action. However, I think such a gambit is unnecessary. I'm positive you'll accept us as a couple, and believe there's a proven psychology behind my way of thinking.'

'You do?' Olivia said.

'Yes,' Grossman replied. He placed his elbows on the table, clasped his hands together, and went on. 'Have you ever heard of Stockholm syndrome?'

She shook her head. 'No, I don't believe I have.'

'Back in 1973,' Grossman said, 'a man call Jan-Erik Olsson took three women and a man hostage during a bank robbery. It failed, but Olsson managed to negotiate the release of a friend called Clark Olofsson from prison.

'Olofsson helped Olsson keep the hostages captive for six days, during which time the criminals treated their captives with kindness. In fact, over the entire period, the men and their prisoners became so close, that when the Stockholm police finally managed to negotiate their release, none of the hostages would testify against them. In fact, they actually raised money for their defence in court. It was even rumoured that a romantic attachment began between Olsson and one of the women.

'You see what I'm getting at, don't you, Olivia?' he continued. 'A case which proves that no human being can live in close proximity to another where kindness exists, without a close bond being formed?'

Olivia didn't think there was any correlation between the case and her present predicament, but decided to play along. 'Yes,' she said. 'I see your point.'

Grossman sat back in his chair with a look of triumph. 'You see, darling? I knew you would.' He gestured to the window. 'Now, what about a little walk tomorrow morning, alongside the stream to the top edge of the property? We don't want you to suffer claustrophobia from being in that tiny little room every day, now, do we?'

Chapter Ten

'Okay, Mark,' Knox said, 'now replay the video we got from Doonan's in Market Street.' The detectives were still gathered around Hathaway's computer, attempting to find out what had happened to Olivia after she arrived at Waverley Bridge.

Hathaway replayed Doonan's video, but neither Olivia herself nor Grossman's RAV4 could be seen.

Knox thought for a moment or two. 'We checked Grossman's DVLA records?'

'Yes, boss,' Hathaway said. 'Two vehicles registered to him since he passed his test in 2019. He became the third registered keeper of a Toyota Corolla in May 2020. His current vehicle, a Toyota RAV4, was registered new in September last year.'

'The Corolla,' Knox said. 'Did he sell it on?'

Hathaway shook his head. 'I'm not sure I checked that, boss.'

'Okay,' Knox said. 'Let's take a look. Tap into the DVLA records again.'

Hathaway navigated to the DVLA website, clicked on Grossman's file, and a record of vehicles registered to him came up on the screen.

The young detective scrolled through the documents until he came to the Corolla's V5C, or log book. 'No record of it being transferred to another owner, boss,' he said.

'Which would have happened had he sold it on?' Knox said.

'Yes, boss.'

'What about insurance?'

'He's got blanket cover from the Royal & General. Insured to drive any non-commercial vehicle.'

'So he could still have the Corolla?' Fulton said.

Hathaway nodded. 'Yes, no record of a transfer of ownership.'

'What are its details, Mark?' Knox asked.

Hathaway studied the screen. 'Dark-blue, four-door saloon, first registered October 2012.' He highlighted the car's registration details and tapped the screen. 'That's the index number.'

'Right,' Knox said. 'Let's see Doonan's tape again.'

A moment later the detectives studied the section of video covering Market Street from the junction of Waverley Bridge to roughly fifty yards from Doonan's entrance. They witnessed a procession of taxis and cars turn from Waverley Bridge into Market Street, all heading east.

'There,' McCann said. 'Other side of the Parcelforce van.'

Hathaway paused the video and the detectives checked the screen.

'Roll it a bit more, Mark,' Knox said, 'the number isn't completely visible.'

Hathaway forwarded the video a couple of seconds, paused, and pointed to the registration number. 'It's our Corolla, all right,' he said.

'The car only appears for a few seconds,' Knox said, pointing to the screen. 'Right behind the van.'

'Aye,' Fulton replied. 'You can make out the driver, but not in any detail. No sign of Olivia.'

'She's drugged,' McCann said. 'Unlikely to be sitting upright in the passenger seat. She'll be in the back.'

Knox nodded and turned to the others. 'It's fair to assume he's picked her up on Waverley Bridge.' He paused. 'Market Street, heading east.'

'Could be going anywhere,' Fulton said.

'No,' McCann replied. 'East or south – and he used the Corolla to buy time. He knew we'd look for the RAV4.'

'Which means he's likely to have parked the four-wheel drive somewhere en route, and transferred from the Corolla,' Knox said. 'Okay,' he added, checking his watch, 'it's 6.30pm, we'll call it a day. Before you go, Mark, get in touch with uniform. Ask them to keep a look out for the Corolla, very likely parked in the suburbs east of the city. Then contact Traffic Scotland, get access to the ANPR CCTV network covering all main routes south and east. We'll pick it up again in the morning.'

* * *

Leckie felt hungry. He glanced at his watch and saw it was 3.25pm, and realised the last time he'd had anything had been breakfast at the Travelodge. He checked the kitchen cupboard again, and saw that in addition to tea bags and dried milk, Billy had left a can of Baxter's lentil soup.

He decided that would keep him going until Frankie had been and he was able to get out and find something more substantial. He heated the soup, poured it into a bowl, and had just finished eating when the doorbell rang.

Leckie checked the peephole and saw a tousle-haired teenager with a document case under his arm.

'Frankie,' Leckie said, opening the door. 'Kirsty gave you the FRG contract?'

'Yes, Mr Leckie,' the youth said hesitantly.

'Well, don't just stand there, son,' Leckie said. 'Come in.'

Frankie followed him into the living room, where Leckie waved to a sideboard. 'Lay the papers over there and I'll get a pen,' he said.

Frankie did so and Leckie retrieved a pen from his inside jacket pocket.

'Kirsty also gave you the builder's contract for Spylaw Road?' he asked.

Frankie rummaged in the document case for a moment and gave Leckie a blank look. 'I was sure I had it in the folder, Mr Leckie,' he said. 'But I can't seem to find it.'

Leckie signed the FRG contract and handed it to the young man. 'Here, son, put this in your document case and don't lose it.' A pause. 'The builder's contract, you're sure you brought it with you?'

Frankie indicated a leather fastening at the top of the folder. 'Strap's a bit loose, Mr Leckie,' he said. 'Might still be in the Lambretta's pannier. I've been over quite a few speed bumps on the way here.'

Leckie grinned. 'Speed bumps, eh? Bit of a waste of time the way you young fellas ride.' Leckie paused. 'Okay Frankie, check the pannier and if you find it bring it in and we'll sort it. If not, don't worry, we'll get Kirsty to print out another copy and I'll deal with it tomorrow.'

Leckie placed the document folder under Frankie's arm. 'But don't lose this under any circumstances – okay? It's important the courier gets it today.'

'No worries, Mr Leckie,' Frankie said. 'I'll take care of it.'

Leckie closed the door after the teenager, and had just returned to the living room when the doorbell rang again. He went to the door and opened it. 'So the builder's contract was in the pannier aft–'

He stopped short when he saw the caller wasn't Frankie, but a well-built man in his late twenties or early thirties. He was dressed in black, and held a pistol in his

right hand, the muzzle of which was aimed at Leckie's
chest.

'Inside,' the man snapped. 'Now!'

Leckie backed into the hallway, his face drained of
colour. 'You're the guy who…'

'Paid you a visit at Spylaw Road?' the man said. 'Aye.
Figured you'd go to ground somewhere, so I kept watch
on your office. Your wee scooter lad pointed me in the
right direction.'

Leckie continued into the living room, the gunman
watching his every move. His retreat halted when his legs
came into contact with an armchair.

He looked down and indicated his jacket. 'The key,' he
said, his voice quaking. 'It's in my jacket pocket.'

The gunman raised the Beretta, centred its sight on
Leckie's forehead, and pulled the trigger…

Chapter Eleven

Knox bade the others goodnight and headed up through
the Old Town via North and South Bridge. He turned left
at East Preston Street, right again at the glass-fronted
Scottish Widows building, and left into Holyrood Park
Road.

A hundred yards short of the entrance to Holyrood Park, he took another left into East Parkside and reversed into the parking bay outside number 139. He let himself into Flat 4, where he changed into a sweatshirt, grey jogging pants and slip-on shoes, then went to the drinks cabinet in the living room, where he poured himself a generous measure of Glenmorangie.

He had only just settled into his favourite armchair when the hands-free phone on the coffee table beside him started ringing.

'Hello, Knox,' he said.

'Guess who?' a female voice replied.

The caller was Lucy Carmichael, the pathologist whom semi-retired Alexander Turley had been standing in for while she was on an exchange visit with the FBI Laboratory Division at Quantico, Virginia.

'Lucy,' Knox said. 'Long time no hear.'

'I tried to reach you before I came over,' Carmichael said. 'But DCI Warburton told me you were in Australia.'

'Yeah,' Knox said. 'Ships that pass in the night.'

Knox had been visiting his son, Jamie, his son's wife, Anne, and granddaughter Lily in Moreton Bay, a suburb of Brisbane, at the beginning of April. His ex-wife, Susan, was there at the same time, staying with her sister only a few streets away.

'Yeah, sorry,' Carmichael said. 'I don't know what you must think of me.'

'Nothing negative, Lucy, I assure you,' Knox said.

'Apt, however, that you said ships that pass in the night,' Carmichael said. 'Considering our history.'

She and Knox had met when she arrived in Edinburgh to take over from Turley in the latter half of 2019. She'd been coming to terms with a split from her husband, whose liaison with another woman had made her cautious about new relationships.

Despite this, she and Knox had embarked on a brief affair, which lasted until the beginning of 2020. Carmichael had then been one of the first to contract Covid and, because of strict no-contact rules, they hadn't seen each other again for several months.

By which time Carmichael had heard from her former husband, George, who'd pleaded for forgiveness and implored her to think again about ending their marriage.

She'd become conflicted and, as a consequence of this and lengthy periods of convalescence due to long Covid, she and Knox had almost ceased contact.

'Nonsense,' Knox said. 'I was glad to hear you're well again.'

'Thanks, Jack,' Carmichael said. 'I still get periods of fatigue, though a lot less now thanks to AXA1125. Lucky I was chosen by Oxford University to participate in their study. It's helped me live almost a normal life.'

'Alex will be pleased,' Knox said. 'He told me you were back on Monday. He sounded relieved.'

Carmichael laughed. 'Yes, he will be, poor man. I was supposed to have taken over from him at the Cowgate three years ago.'

'Don't worry,' Knox said. 'It's a bluff. He's in his element.' He paused. 'So, how are you getting on with all this CSI stuff – learning anything new?'

'You'd have to see it to believe it, Jack,' Carmichael said. 'They've one of the most advanced pathology labs in the world.'

'Yeah?'

'Yes,' she said. 'I paid a visit to the body farm yesterday – absolutely amazing.'

'Body farm?'

'Yes,' Carmichael replied. 'It was begun in 1981 to study human decomposition. The site covers two and a half acres. Human donors are buried, partially covered, or left out in the elements, which allows forensic anthropologists to study how bodies break down under different conditions.

'When the burial place of a corpse is discovered, for example, pathologists map it on a grid of twine and stakes, then scrape away layers of dirt, which are sifted for clues. We were also shown techniques on how heat affects dentistry, and how maggots reveal clues about the recently deceased.'

'Sounds unmissable.'

'No, really, it was totally fascinating.'

'But not for the squeamish, eh?' Knox said.

'Come on, Jack, you've seen more than your share in your time in the job, surely?'

'Under sufferance, Lucy. And from as far a distance as possible.'

'Go on, you're pulling my leg.'

'No, really,' Knox said. 'Ask Alex.'

Carmichael laughed. 'Well, I met a senior lecturer at the forensic pathology laboratory yesterday, Emily Sutton. She's got a book out called, *Understanding Forensic Pathology*. I'll bring you back a copy.'

'Look forward to it,' Knox said.

'I'll ring you too when I get home, Jack, okay?'

'Promise?'

'I promise.'

* * *

The next morning Knox left McCann and Hathaway to review Traffic Scotland's ANPR footage whilst he and Fulton went to interview Charlie O'Dowd.

The former raider's bungalow was situated in Priestfield Terrace, a ten-minute drive from the office. As the detectives arrived, a man was cutting the hedge outside with a trimmer. He turned, regarded them with curiosity for a moment, then switched off the machine.

'Mr O'Dowd?' Knox said as they exited the car.

'Aye,' the man said. 'Who's asking?'

Knox and Fulton held up their warrant cards. 'Detective Inspector Knox and Detective Sergeant Fulton,'

Knox said, and nodded to the house. 'Could we talk for a minute?'

O'Dowd opened the gate, set down the trimmer, and waved to the door.

'Aye,' he said. 'Come in.'

The detectives followed him into a short hallway, where he waved to a door on the right. 'Go inside and park yourselves on the settee,' he said, and nodded to the end of the hall. 'I'll wash my hands and join you in a minute.'

A few moments later, he came into the sitting room, drying his hands on a towel. 'So,' he said, 'what's it all about?'

'We're investigating the murders of three men at a house on Spylaw Road on Monday evening,' Knox said. 'The property belongs to a Mr Hugh Leckie.'

'Shug Leckie?' O'Dowd said. 'He was killed?'

'No,' Knox replied. 'Mr Leckie wasn't in the property at the time. The men were his employees.'

O'Dowd shook his head. 'Strangers to me, whoever they are. I've not seen Shug since the day of the trial. No doubt you know about the George Street robbery?'

'Yes, Mr O'Dowd,' Knox said. 'We do.'

O'Dowd looked directly at Knox for a long moment. 'Then you'll also know I've kept my nose clean since, Inspector,' he said.

'I'm aware of that, Mr O'Dowd,' Knox said. 'However, there's a possibility Mr Leckie may have been a target. We're here to ask your help in that regard.'

'I told you,' O'Dowd said. 'I've not seen Shug since we were in court. And, in any case, why should I have any enmity towards him?'

Knox cleared his throat. 'A box of diamonds went missing during the raid,' he said, 'which was never recovered.'

O'Dowd made a face. 'Aye, I remember that being reported in the papers at the time. Absolute bollocks, if you'll pardon the expression. The haul was taken directly to Leckie's place in Gorebridge. All of us saw the goods. There were no diamonds.'

'Your brother Andy was unhappy with his cut, though?' Fulton said. 'Wasn't it through him that you and the others were caught?'

O'Dowd shook his head mournfully. 'Aye,' he said. 'Andy was a silly laddie. We all agreed his cut in advance – a half-share of what the rest got. Since he was the driver, he was taking less risk. Andy was fine with that, by the way.

'Fact is he didn't grass us up, contrary to what some believe. We got caught because of his stupidity. He gave his wife a gold necklace, which she wore to a local pub a few nights later. Then some envious arsehole reported it. One of your senior dicks threatened my brother… can't remember his name.'

'DCI Fletcher,' Knox said.

'Aye, Fletcher. Told Andy if he didn't talk he'd serve fifteen years. He couldn't take that; his boy was little more than a toddler at the time – would have been in his late teens by the time he got out.'

'When we interviewed Mr Leckie, he told us your brother had died?' Knox said.

'Aye, three years ago,' O'Dowd said. 'Liver cancer. Took him in four months. Just as Coronavirus hit and lockdowns came into force. Cathie – his wife – was allowed to see him in hospital, but even her visits were restricted. Only a few of us were permitted at his funeral, too. Cathie told me Leckie sent a wreath and phoned her to convey his condolences.'

Knox gave an understanding nod.

'And before you ask where I was on Monday evening,' O'Dowd added, 'it was the Minto Hotel in Minto Street. Quarterly meeting of the Southside Curling Club, of which I happen to be chairman of. Any of the members will confirm I was there between 7pm and 11pm.'

Knox stood up and Fulton followed his lead. 'Fine, Mr O'Dowd,' he said. 'I think that covers it. Thanks for your cooperation.'

'No bother,' O'Dowd said, opening the sitting room door. 'I'll see you both out and get back to the hedge-cutting. I promised the wife I'd get it done before she gets back from the supermarket.'

* * *

Knox switched on his iPhone as they got back in the car and it gave a loud beep. He opened a text message, which read:

Jack: proceed to 46 Balmoral Place ASAP. Hugh Leckie shot dead. DI Murray, DS Beattie & pathologist in attendance – Warburton.

Knox showed the message to Fulton and placed the mobile on the dash bracket.

'How the hell can that have happened?' Fulton said. 'You warned him to be careful.'

Knox shook his head. 'Aye, not careful enough, apparently,' he replied, highlighting a number on the iPhone. 'I'll ring ahead, get Murray to give us a heads-up while we're on our way. It'll save time.'

The ringtone sounded on the speakers, and a moment later Murray answered, 'Jack?'

'Just received Warburton's message, Ed,' Knox replied. 'Bill and I were doing an interview.'

'Aye, the DCI told me.'

'Where was he found?' Knox asked.

'On the floor near the living-room fireplace. Discovered by his office boy, a seventeen-year-old called Frank Reynolds. Told uniform he took a contract to Leckie yesterday afternoon, but forgot a second paper, which Leckie asked him to bring down this morning. The crime scene's a bit contaminated, I'm afraid – the laddie threw up in the hallway.'

'The shooter – same MO?'

'Yeah. Alex's taken a quick look; appears he was shot in the head.'

'The office boy has a car?'

'No, a Lambretta scooter.'

'Uniform asked if he was aware of anything unusual?'

'To ascertain if he was followed, you mean?'

'Yes,' said Knox.

'He told the constable that he never noticed.'

The roads into town were quiet and Knox had made good time. 'Okay, Ed, thanks,' he said. 'Be with you shortly.'

A few minutes later, Knox turned into Balmoral Place, found a vacant space, and parked. The detectives put on anti-contaminant coveralls, climbed the stairs to number forty-six, and entered the hallway.

'Oh, my God,' Fulton said, grimacing. 'What a pen and ink.'

DS Liz Beattie came out of the kitchen at that moment and pointed to newspapers covering a section of carpet. 'The young lad who discovered the body was sick,' she said. 'Avoid the newspapers.'

'Good advice in more ways than one,' Fulton said. His expression had changed and he tipped Beattie a wink.

'No, I meant they're covering–' she started to say.

'It's okay, Liz,' Knox interrupted. 'Bill's joking.' He gestured to the end of the hallway. 'Ed and Alex in there?'

Beattie nodded. 'Yes.' She thumbed towards the kitchen. 'So far I've found prints on a work surface next to the cooker, but I'm inclined to think they're Leckie's. More on a half-empty mug of tea.'

Knox gave her an acknowledging nod, and the detectives carried on to the living room.

They entered and found DI Murray hunkered near an armchair, inspecting the carpet with a UV light. Turley was a couple of feet away, using a small scalpel to examine Leckie's head injury.

Knox returned Murray's nod as the pathologist turned, registered their presence, and tapped gently on Leckie's body. 'DCI Warburton told me this was supposed to have been the deceased's safe house. Didn't turn out that way, did it?'

'No, indeed, Alex,' Knox agreed. 'Pity he had a contract to sign. The killer's been watching his office; followed the boy here.'

Murray held up a cartridge shell with his thumb and index finger. 'Same as yesterday,' he said, '9mm shell. I'd guess a Beretta.'

'Find anything else?' Knox asked.

Murray nodded to the entrance. 'There's a couple of footprints on the flooring near the door. Looks like the same pattern we found at Spylaw.' Murray paused. 'But I did find something that may be of significance.'

'Go on,' Knox said.

'Fragments of bone, a couple more than 2mm across. If we're lucky, they might have the killer's DNA on them.' He glanced at Turley. 'Alex?'

The pathologist pointed towards Leckie's prostrate corpse. 'The bullet tore into the supraorbital ridge, the section of skull just above the eyes,' he said. 'Unlike at Spylaw Road, though, the killer was nearer. From where Ed found the fragments and the position of the deceased, I'd say around three feet.'

Turley tapped his brow. 'This particular part of the skull is hard, very hard. Given the killer's proximity, I'd say there's a fair chance some of the fragments Ed found may have struck the shooter first.'

'Enough to do damage?' Knox asked.

'Yes,' Turley confirmed. 'Look for minor injuries on the face of your suspect. Tiny lacerations, like he's cut himself shaving.'

Knox dipped his head in acknowledgement. 'That could prove very helpful.' He paused and looked around. 'Okay, thanks, Alex, Ed. We'll get on and leave you to it. We've yet to speak to Thomas Salter, the last of Leckie's former cohorts. Never know what it'll turn up.'

Chapter Twelve

'One point I should like to make crystal clear before we take our little jaunt, Olivia,' Grossman was saying, 'is that you must stay no farther than arm's length from me at all times.'

He and his hostage were seated at the sitting-room table and had just finished breakfast.

'No doubt you've had a peek out of the window in your bedroom recess,' he continued. 'And seen the woods at the top of the meadow. These mark the boundary of my property. No doubt, too, you noticed the stream from the hills that meanders through the trees on the right. On the other side of there is a single-track road.

'We'll hold to the treeline on our walk, since that affords the most cover from prying eyes. However – and I must emphasise this – if we encounter anyone who attempts to engage us in conversation, I want you to say nothing – is that understood?'

Olivia put down her knife and fork and dabbed her mouth with a napkin. 'Of course,' she replied. Keep up the masquerade, she thought to herself. *The more he believes you've accepted the situation, the more likely he is to let his guard down.*

'Okay,' Grossman said. 'Better put a warm jumper on under your coat. It may be mid-April, but it can be very chilly here, particularly in the mornings. I'll put away the breakfast things and be along in a minute.'

Olivia went back to her room, put on her jumper and parka, and five minutes later Grossman popped his head around the door.

'Ready, then?' he asked.

'Yes,' Olivia replied.

'Okay, let's go,' Grossman said.

She followed him along the passageway to the rear door, where he took a keyring from his pocket, made a show of selecting one of the keys and inserting it into the lock, and opened the door.

'Remember, Olivia,' he said. 'Stay close at all times.'

They went outside where she waited until he'd locked up, then went with him along a narrow path towards the trees.

Olivia inhaled the cool, fresh morning air, and immediately felt better. The three days she'd spent in the stale confines of the bedroom had been both depressing and demoralising. But now, out in the open, she felt a sense of freedom. Her spirits continued to soar for a few brief moments, then reality dawned. She wasn't quite free – yet.

A few minutes later they arrived at a path near the trees. She saw the stream clearly from here and, a short distance beyond, a single-track road which ran parallel.

The path grew steeper, and before long they were only a short distance from the wide grove of oak and elder she'd seen from the alcove window.

The trees bordering the stream were farther apart now, leaving gaps that allowed her to see the road more clearly. Grossman began to pick up his stride, and she felt slightly out of breath keeping up.

He noticed this and said, 'Sorry, darling. I'd forgotten. You must be a bit out of condition being cooped up in the house.' He slackened his pace, and added, 'I'll go easier.'

Olivia gestured to the hills beyond the woods. 'That narrow road,' she said, 'does it go anywhere?'

Grossman smiled. 'Still wondering where you are, eh, Olivia?' He paused. 'I told you, darling, we're in a very remote area.'

He'd only just said this when he froze in his tracks. He raised a hand, indicating her to stop. A moment later, Olivia heard the sound of a diesel engine. She looked to the road and saw a white camper van approach from behind. The driver appeared to have seen them, too, as he began to slow.

'Remember what I told you,' Grossman hissed. 'Stay by my side and say nothing.'

The camper van came to a stop. Olivia saw the driver was a man in his late sixties, his passenger a woman about the same age. The man exited the vehicle and looked in Grossman's direction.

'Excuse me,' he said in a pronounced Yorkshire accent. 'My sat nav looks to have packed up. Could you tell me if I'm on the right road for Langholm and the A7?'

'Yes,' Grossman said pleasantly. 'About another ten miles.'

'Thanks,' the man said. 'Is it single-track all the way?'

'Afraid so,' Grossman said. 'Fair number of passing places. You can see them well ahead – plenty of time to pull in. There's a few gated cattle grids en route. Take care to close them after you.'

The man gave a look of resignation. 'Lad back in Newcastleton told me it were a short cut. Wish I'd gone via Canonbie now.' He got back into the camper van. 'Ah well… thanks again.'

After he'd continued on his way, Grossman turned to Olivia. 'There's always a few unused to the single-track road. And inevitably one or two who like to make sure they're headed in the right direction.'

'Canonbie and Langholm,' Olivia said. 'They're towns in the Scottish Borders, aren't they?'

Grossman gave a little laugh. 'My secret's out now, isn't it, darling? Yes, the cottage is three miles west of Newcastleton.'

His expression changed and became serious. 'You kept quiet, Olivia. Yet I'm sure you were tempted to say something, which would have been unwise.'

Of course I was tempted, Olivia thought. But her instincts told her now wasn't the time. Grossman had been at her elbow throughout, and the couple were on the other side of the stream.

If she'd said anything, it would have been easy for Grossman to have ignored the man, seized her arm, and hustled her on.

She could have screamed, of course, but the camper van driver might have wondered what he'd stumbled into. Some kind of domestic dispute? A neurotic woman, perhaps? There was every chance he just might have shrugged his shoulders and carried on.

No. She had to choose a moment when Grossman's attention was diverted long enough to enable her to make a clean break.

But the walk had been valuable in that she now knew where she was. She had a better idea of her surroundings, too.

If she was lucky and he could be distracted long enough, she'd dash for the woods at the top of the meadow. It would be easier for her to hide and lie in wait until she heard a vehicle. All she had to do then was break cover, cross the stream, and get help…

* * *

Redford Way was situated in the middle of a row of semi-detached houses in a new-build housing estate at the western edge of the city.

Knox waited while a couple of refuse collectors rolled bins from either side of the street to a waiting truck and steered them into the arms of its hoisting mechanism, which lifted and emptied them before depositing them back onto the roadway.

'Trust us to pick an uplift day,' Fulton said.

Knox gestured to cars parked on both sides of the street. 'Inconsiderate parking,' he said, and nodded to the refuse truck. 'The driver's got a bad enough job manoeuvring a wagon that size through these narrow streets.'

'Aye, you've a point,' Fulton said, then indicated the truck, which had begun to move. 'We can get on now, though.'

Knox drove another hundred yards, and came to a stop. 'Seventy-six,' he said, glancing at the house. 'Looks quiet. I wonder if he's in.'

'Only one way to find out,' Fulton said.

The detectives exited the car, walked up a narrow path, and Knox rang the doorbell. Twenty seconds passed, and Knox thumbed the buzzer again.

'One of the downsides of the element of surprise,' Fulton said, 'is that sometimes you draw a blank.'

Knox caught a faint sound from within and pushed the doorbell a third time. 'No, I hear something,' he said.

Seconds later, he and Fulton heard the sound of feet padding down the stairs, then a key turned and the door opened.

The man who answered had a dishevelled look, with a mop of hair which covered his forehead. 'Yeah?' he said.

'Thomas Salter?' Knox asked.

Knox reached inside his pocket to retrieve his warrant card, but the man raised a hand.

'It's okay,' he said. 'I know you're cops. Who else would it be at this time in the morning?'

Fulton glanced at his watch. 'It's 10.37am,' he said. 'Not that early.'

'It is for me,' the man said.

'You *are* Thomas Salter?' Knox repeated.

'Yeah,' the man said, opening the door wider. 'I suppose you better come in before the neighbours' curtains start twitching.'

The detectives went inside, where Salter waved to a room off the hallway. 'In here,' he said. 'I had a bit of a nightcap. I'll clear up later.'

The detectives entered the room and Knox saw he was referring to a half dozen empty beer cans, which were strewn across a coffee table.

Salter indicated chairs placed at a dining table near the window. 'Take the weight off,' he said.

The detectives pulled out a couple of chairs and sat down, and Salter took a chair opposite.

'So,' he said. 'What can I do for you?'

'Hugh Leckie,' Knox replied.

'What about him?'

'He was shot dead yesterday,' Knox said. 'And three men who worked for him were murdered on Monday.'

Salter drew a thumb across his unshaven chin. 'Really?' he said casually. 'Pity, but I can't see what that's got to do with me.'

'The George Street safe box raid back in 2003,' Knox said.

Salter shook his head. 'Christ, man, that was twenty years ago.'

'You've seen Leckie since?'

'No, why should I? We did our time, didn't we?' A pause. 'In separate prisons, I might add. Gone straight since then, haven't I? Lilian, my wife– no, sorry, ex-wife; she divorced me five years ago – made me take the pledge.' He nodded to the empty cans. 'To go straight, I mean, not give up the booze.' He studied Knox for a long moment, and continued, 'You've checked your files, you know I've kept a clean sheet?'

Knox ignored the question. 'When was the last time you saw Leckie?' he asked.

Salter thought for a moment. 'At the divvy in Gorebridge,' he said.

'You took equal shares?' Knox asked.

'With the exception of Andy O'Dowd, aye. I think he got a half. Bastard didn't even deserve that, since he was the one who grassed us up.'

'You were happy with the way the haul was divided?'

'Yeah, why?'

'There's a rumour that a box of diamonds went missing. Worth quite a bundle. Know anything about it?'

'I don't think so,' Salter said.

Knox noticed that rivulets of sweat were beginning to trickle down the sides of his temples.

'It was all over the papers at the time,' Knox said. 'You mean to tell me it was never discussed?'

Salter shrugged and pushed hair back off his forehead. 'Not in my presence it wasn't.'

Fulton cleared his throat loudly. Knox saw him tap his forehead and clear his throat again. He looked back at Salter and saw several minute cuts beneath the hairline.

'Can you tell me where you were yesterday, Mr Salter?' he said. 'Afternoon and evening?'

'Afternoon *and* evening?' Salter asked.

'Yes.'

Salter stroked his chin again. 'Afternoon, here in the house. I rose late, had something to eat and took a shower. Left around five, five-thirty. There was a darts match scheduled for seven at the Hunter's Tryst, my local. I knew I'd be in for a lengthy session so I left the car and took a taxi. Arrived around six. That was me until… well, I'm honestly not sure, ten-thirty? Eleven? Darts night is an excuse for a piss-up, really.'

'You took a taxi back home?'

'Aye.'

'Anyone vouch for seeing you there?'

Salter made a face. 'You serious?' he said. 'Only about a dozen regulars on the darts team. And the bar staff, of course.'

'The darts team,' Knox said. 'Do you know their names?'

'Tommy, Ally, Peter…' Salter shook his head. 'Hell, I can't remember them all.'

'What about surnames?'

Salter shook his head. 'They're guys I play darts with on Tuesday nights. I might talk to one or two over a pint at other times but, no, I don't know their surnames.'

Knox pointed to Salter's head. 'I couldn't help noticing you have a series of injuries. Mind telling me how you got them?'

Salter ran his fingers over the cuts. 'Oh, these?' he said. He hesitated. 'I was a bit legless when I left the pub. I think I stumbled on my way to the taxi. Didn't realise I'd banged myself up that badly.'

'Do you own a gun, Mr Salter?' Knox asked.

'Eh?' Salter replied.

'Do you own a gun?' Knox repeated.

Salter's eyes flitted from Knox to Fulton, and back to Knox. 'No, of course I don't,' he replied.

Knox took out his iPhone. 'I think you're lying, Mr Salter, and I intend phoning to ask for a search warrant. So, I repeat, do you own a gun?'

Salter was sweating profusely now. He remained silent for several moments, then said, 'The Falklands.'

'Come again?' Knox said.

'The Falklands War – I was in the Paras. We were issued with Browning Hi-Power pistols as a sidearm before the advance on San Carlos. I smuggled mine home in my rucksack.' He paused and added, 'I wasn't the only one.'

'Where is it now?' Knox asked.

'In my bedroom.'

'Where in your bedroom?'

'Top of the wardrobe, in a Tesco carrier bag.'

Knox nodded to Fulton, who took a pair of nitrile gloves from his pocket and left the room, returning a minute later with the weapon zipped into an evidence bag.

'See anything else?' Knox asked his colleague.

'No, boss,' Fulton replied.

'Have you ammunition for the weapon?' he asked Salter.

'No,' Salter replied dryly.

'What calibre does it take?'

'It's 9mm.'

Knox glanced at Fulton, who gave an almost imperceptible nod, then turned back to Salter. 'Mr Salter,' he said, 'I'm arresting you under section 1 of the Criminal Justice Scotland Act 2016 for the suspected murder of Hugh Leckie.

'Other charges may follow subsequent to our investigations. You don't have to make any statement, but anything you say will be noted and may be used in evidence.'

Chapter Thirteen

Soon after Knox and Fulton had left to interview Salter, Hathaway logged into Traffic Scotland's video recordings for the weekend beginning 10pm Friday 14 April. McCann sat at his side, the officers having set the automatic number plate recognition to pick up sightings of the registration number of Grossman's Toyota RAV4.

A few minutes earlier they'd got their first lead when they received a call from the Traffic division to say Grossman's Corolla had been located in Edinburgh's suburbs. It was found parked in Northfield Road, to the east of the city.

'The boss was right,' Hathaway said. 'He's transferred to the RAV4.'

McCann pointed to the screen. 'So it's the A1,' she said.

'I'll activate the ANPR from Milton Road,' Hathaway said.

The desktop pinged and a section of video came up on the screen. It showed Grossman's vehicle passing a vantage point at a busy crossroads where the A1 intersected Duddingston Park South.

The young detective clicked the mouse a second time. The screen blanked momentarily, then a message flashed "Searching…"

A moment later the computer pinged again and a section of video captioned "Milton Link/Edinburgh Bypass" came on the screen.

'We're still on the A1,' Hathaway said.

'He's heading south?' McCann asked.

'Maybe not,' Hathaway said. 'There's another big intersection coming up. The city bypass leads off, and after that there's two possible choices: the A68 and A7.'

'Both routes to the Scottish Borders?' McCann said.

'Yes, the A7 more to the west; Carlisle, the M6.'

The detectives watched the ANPR follow the RAV4 through a series of vantage points, then the vehicle took the A7 via Galashiels, Hawick and finally, Langholm.

'Traffic Scotland's cameras take us as far as Longtown,' Hathaway explained. 'After that, we'd have to switch to the English network.'

'Where's the next CCTV?' McCann asked.

'Canonbie,' Hathaway replied. 'The last of Traffic Scotland's cameras is a couple of miles from the English border.'

They studied the screen. It pinged again and the caption read "Canonbie".

The vantage point of the camera was at a well-lit petrol station. The detectives saw Grossman behind the wheel and Olivia in the passenger seat.

'Look,' McCann said. 'Olivia. We couldn't see her in the Market Street footage. He must have moved her.'

'Would've looked suspicious if he'd left her in the back for any length of time,' Hathaway said. 'Still slumped in her seat, though.'

'Wouldn't necessarily draw attention,' McCann said. 'Anyone would think she was sleeping.' She pointed to a caption on the screen, which read "End of ANPR sightings".

'What does that mean?' she asked.

'It's where the trail ends,' Hathaway replied.

'You mean—'

Hathaway cut in. 'Grossman pulled off the A7,' he said. 'Somewhere between Canonbie and the next ANPR point.'

* * *

'You told us you had no ammunition for the Browning,' Knox was saying. 'Yet officers who carried out a search of your house found a box with eighteen cartridges. How do you explain that?'

He and Fulton were sitting opposite Salter at a plain metal table in Interview Room 2 at Gayfield Square Police Station. Also present was Salter's legal representative, Alan Strang, who was seated next to his client.

'I'd forgotten they were there,' Salter said.

'Eighteen bullets in an old tobacco tin wrapped in foil and stuffed at the back of a dresser? It just slipped your mind you'd put them there?'

'I told you, I brought them back from the Falklands,' Salter said. 'They've been there since I was demobbed.'

'When were you demobbed?' Fulton asked.

'1982.'

'Where were you living at the time?' Knox said.

'With my parents – Coatfield Lane in Leith.'

'Where did you live after you got married?

'Manderston Street.'

'And you live at Redford Way now,' Knox said. 'Not counting staying with your parents, you've moved twice, and on each occasion taken both cartridges and gun with you – and you forgot they were there?'

Salter shrugged, but said nothing.

'You told us you were at the Hunter's Tryst public house between the hours of six and eleven o'clock last night–'

'Ten-thirty,' Strang interrupted. 'The notes of your interview this morning state my client told you he wasn't sure. He thought it might have been ten-thirty *or* eleven.'

Knox gave the lawyer a tetchy look. 'For the purposes of establishing where your client was,' he said, 'it's unimportant.'

Strang looked smug. 'Details *are* important, Detective Inspector. We must get them right.'

'Okay,' Knox said, looking Strang directly in the eye. 'Between six and ten-thirty.' A pause. 'The point of my question was to establish the veracity of your client's alibi.'

Knox turned back to Salter. 'Fact is, Mr Salter, officers visited the Hunter's Tryst a little over an hour ago. The workers they spoke to were the same staff who were on duty last night. On being shown your photograph, they acknowledged that you were a regular customer. None, however, could say with certainty they remember seeing you last night.'

'That's bullshit,' Salter said. 'The darts team, myself included, were buying drinks all night.'

'Ah, yes, the darts team,' Knox said, 'you weren't able to give us surnames. We are of course continuing to make inquiries to track them down. In the meantime, your alibi is looking a little shaky.'

Salter turned to Strang. 'You gonna let him get away with this?' he said. 'I was where I said I was, playing darts. The bar staff were busy, so maybe they don't remember. But the darts guys are regulars, they're bound to confirm I was there.'

Strang addressed Knox. 'You'll continue to make inquiries until you discover who these men are?'

'Of course,' Knox replied. 'Meantime, our ballistics team are checking the Browning pistol and forensics are comparing DNA found at the scene with that of your client.'

Salter emitted an audible sigh and gave Knox a look of disgust. 'You really think I shot Leckie?'

'I'm sorry, Mr Salter, but until we examine the weapon, complete the forensics, *and* speak to someone who can verify your presence at the Hunter's Tryst last night, we can't assume anything. For this reason we have to remand you in custody.'

'The COPFS order,' Strang said, 'when does it expire?'

'We can hold your client without charge for another twelve hours,' Knox said, then checked his watch and turned to the recorder. 'Interview terminated at 1.35pm.'

* * *

After a uniformed officer led Salter away, Knox and Fulton returned to the office, where they were intercepted by Warburton.

'Can I have a word, Jack?' he asked.

'Sir,' Knox replied.

'It's the ACC,' Warburton said a minute or two later, when he and Knox were seated in his office. 'Breathing down my neck over the Ledbetter girl. Her father's unhappy we haven't located her yet.'

Knox explained that CCTV revealed that Grossman had switched vehicles, the Corolla had been found at Northfield Road, and that ANPR had tracked his RAV4 to Canonbie.

'No sightings beyond that?' Warburton said.

'No, sir,' Knox confirmed.

'DS McCann's been in touch with an Inspector Laing at our Hawick office,' Knox continued. 'Asked him to check CCTV in garages, pubs and the like between Canonbie and the English border, see if we can pinpoint where he went off-road.'

'There's a possibility he changed vehicles a second time?' Warburton said.

'Can't rule it out, sir,' Knox replied. 'Grossman's been very thorough in planning the abduction, he was aware we'd track him.'

'You think he's gone to ground in the Borders?'

'DS McCann asked Laing to keep a look out for the Toyota, to cover that possibility,' Knox replied. 'If it's found, he'll ask around, see if anyone saw anything.'

'Do you think Olivia's in danger?' Warburton asked.

Knox shook his head. 'Grossman was caught shoplifting at the age of eleven,' he said. 'A psychiatric report at the time revealed he suffered from OCD; also found he was unstable. From what I understand, he's infatuated with Olivia, even though she told him on several occasions she didn't reciprocate his feelings. To answer your question, sir, no, I don't think she's in danger as long as he thinks there's a possibility she might reconsider. If the situation should change, however...'

Warburton gave Knox a despondent look. 'Bloody catch-22, isn't it?'

'Pretty much, sir, yes.'

'Okay, all we can hope for is that Hawick Police find something to put us on the right track.' Warburton remained silent for a long moment, then added, 'Any joy with the Leckie case?'

Knox brought him up to date with his investigations, and concluded, 'Naturally, we're waiting on DNA and forensics. DI Murray's promised to get them to us ASAP.'

'Salter,' Warburton said. 'You think he's guilty?'

Knox shook his head. 'Can't honestly say. I'm confident we've spoken to the killer, though. I just don't know who he is yet.'

Warburton placed his hands on the table and stood up. 'Okay, Jack,' he said, 'promise you'll pull out all the stops on the Ledbetter case?'

'Yes, sir,' Knox replied. 'You have my word on it.'

Chapter Fourteen

It rained the next morning and Olivia worried that Grossman might call off their walk. But by breakfast it had almost ceased, and by eleven the sky was cloudless.

As he cleared away the dishes, Grossman said, 'I thought we'd go to the top of the property today, where the woods are, via a track paralleling the fence on the south side. I don't want motorists interrupting our walk. Of course, it means we'll be out in the open, more easily seen from the road. But, as I say, less chance of anyone stopping to ask directions.'

Shortly afterwards they left the house and, instead of turning right towards the stream as they'd done on Tuesday, they took a path bordering the fence on the opposite side.

Grossman waved to their surroundings and asked, 'What do you think of it?'

'It's lovely,' Olivia replied. 'Quiet and peaceful.'

The shadow of a smile played over his lips. 'A bit too quiet, perhaps? You prefer the city?'

'I do like Edinburgh,' she replied. 'And working there, of course. But it's nice to have such pretty country only a short drive away.'

'For a weekend, you mean? Can't see yourself living here on a permanent basis?'

'Maybe not.'

Grossman laughed. 'I see I've my work cut out. It's going to take me some time to get you used to your new environment.' He laughed again. 'Not to worry, Olivia darling, we'll make a country girl of you yet.'

Olivia felt anger well at the preposterousness of his assumption, and struggled in vain to suppress it. 'Back to your Stockholm theory again,' she retorted, 'you do realise I'm here against my will? That what you're doing is unlawful?'

Grossman stopped and glared at her, his face reddening. 'Okay,' he said, grabbing her arm. 'Back to the house. Your privileges are curtailed. I thought you were coming round to my way of thinking, but I see I'm mistaken.'

'I say there!' A deep baritone voice sounded out from the opposite side of the meadow.

Olivia turned and saw a man in his mid-thirties standing a short distance away. 'Forgive me,' he continued. 'I've a flat tyre and seem to have mislaid my jack. You don't happen to have one, do you?'

If Grossman had been annoyed before, he was positively apoplectic now. 'This is private property,' he exclaimed. 'You're on my land.'

'Hang on, old chap,' the man countered. 'I'm only asking a favour.'

Grossman let go of Olivia's arm and pointed in the direction of the stream. 'You're on *private* property,' he repeated. 'Bugger off!'

He stepped aside and extended his arm to emphasise his point, which was all the opportunity Olivia needed. She turned on her heels, and began sprinting towards the woods.

Grossman swung around, his attentions divided between his fleeing hostage and the trespasser. 'Stop, Olivia,' he shouted. 'Stop!'

'Not very popular, are you, old boy?' the man said. 'I'm not surprised.' Then, as Grossman turned back to face him, he added, 'It's okay, I'm going.'

Olivia meanwhile was halfway to the top of the meadow, the woods fifty yards away.

Moments later she arrived at the treeline, scrambled through thick undergrowth, and was soon deep into the woods.

She kept going, determined to put as much distance between herself and Grossman as possible. After a few minutes of hard running, however, she was struggling for breath. She came to a stop, leaned against an old sycamore, and felt as if her heart was about to burst.

Several more minutes passed before her heart rate returned to normal, her breathing steady.

The thick canopy created a semi-darkness that Olivia's eyes were only beginning to adjust to. If Grossman *was* following, he'd have a hard time finding her. Thick bracken, leaves and fragments of branches made it noisy underfoot which, although advantageous for a pursuer, gave her plenty of warning, too. Olivia strained her ears, but apart from birdsong and the scurrying of small animals, she heard nothing.

She began to contemplate her next move. She must be somewhere in the middle of the wood; from the recess window, she'd estimated its width at around a third of a mile.

If Grossman hadn't followed – and that appeared to be the case – then what would he do next?

He knew she would have to exit cover at some point, take to the hills and head in the direction of the A7.

Another option would be to traverse to a point near the single-track road and listen for a vehicle, then break cover and seek help.

How was Grossman likely to react? His advantage was that he knew the country and had access to a four-wheel-drive.

Olivia mulled over the pros and cons. The first option was to make for Langholm. If she attempted this, she'd be largely in the open, as the country appeared to be pasture land which, although it supported cattle and sheep, was largely desolate.

This was evidenced by Grossman's caution to the camper van driver to close cattle-grid gates on the single-track road.

Large tracts of open land and bare hills meant she'd be highly visible for most of the trek, too and Grossman could easily drive off-road.

The second option was to wait until nightfall. *I'd be almost impossible to find in the dark, wouldn't I?* But that option had a considerable downside. In this sort of landscape, there would be innumerable gullies, small ravines and culverts, and it would be all too easy to break a leg or suffer some other sort of injury. No, walking ten miles in the dark was out of the question.

Which left her with option number three: traverse the woods to a point near the road, wait until she heard a vehicle, then run towards it and summon help.

The danger in this was that by now Grossman would have taken to his Toyota and be watching on the road.

If she could stay under cover and get close enough, however, it would be easy to identify Grossman's car.

Olivia kept pondering his likely strategy. She reckoned he'd watch the fields west of the wood, where she'd likely emerge if she were heading for Langholm. There would be no need for him to leave the Toyota if he saw her, as he could simply switch to the vehicle's four-wheel drive and cover the ground in minutes.

Alternatively, if she dashed from the trees with the aim of attracting a driver, he'd have that covered, too. He'd be able to cut out another vehicle before it came anywhere near her – before she was able to make her predicament known.

There was one other possibility, however. What if he thought she'd already carried on into the hills?

If Grossman believed she'd covered more ground than he'd initially anticipated, he'd take to the road and drive five or more miles before he realised his mistake.

By which time, if she was lucky, another vehicle might just come along and save the day. For that to work, however, she had to make sure he was gone in the first place.

She began heading east, picking her way through dense undergrowth. Finally the trees thinned, and she found herself at the edge of the woods, the road a hundred yards distant.

At that moment, the sound of a diesel engine cut into her thoughts. She looked to the road and saw a light-blue Land Rover picking up speed as it passed in the direction of Langholm.

Damn, she thought. *If only the driver had been going a little slower or I'd heard the vehicle earlier, I could have run over in time to flag him down.*

Olivia reckoned it must be getting on for an hour since she'd made her bid for freedom, and was curious why Grossman hadn't acted as she predicted.

Using the trees for cover, she continued until she had a view of the cottage, and saw the reason why: the garage doors were open. She hadn't heard or seen his RAV4 pass, but it must have been before she arrived at her present position.

She carried on towards the stream, crossed some stepping stones, and surveyed her surroundings. The entrance to the cottage was three hundred yards in the direction of Newcastleton. A gravel drive led to the door, which was fronted by a porch.

The entrance gate was open, further evidence that Grossman had departed. But when, and how far along was he likely to check?

She thought earlier it might be as far as five miles, more ground than she could realistically have covered on foot. If so, he was likely to stop frequently, take a pair of field glasses, and survey the surrounding countryside.

That could take anything from thirty minutes to an hour, so he could return any time now. If she did hear a car, she'd better make sure it wasn't his. For this reason, she retraced her steps to a point where the trees gave cover, yet allowed her enough time to reach the road.

She arrived at a point where the stream intersected the woods, and took shelter in a grove of birch trees.

A few minutes later, her heart leapt when she heard a vehicle approach from the direction of Langholm. It drew nearer, and Olivia saw it was another Land Rover, light-blue like the one she'd seen earlier. It might even be the same one, since there were bound to be farmers in the area looking after the sheep she'd seen dotted around the hillsides.

She ran towards the road, waving her arms, and for an awful moment thought the driver wasn't going to stop. Then suddenly the vehicle slowed and came to a halt several yards away.

The driver wore a flat checked cap, but she wasn't able see his face, as he leaned towards the passenger footwell on her approach, as if retrieving something.

The driver's door opened and Olivia stood rooted to the spot, her mouth agape… Grossman!

She barely had time to register the fact when he leapt from the vehicle, grabbed her wrist, and Olivia felt a sharp prick in her upper arm.

'Another little shot of ketamine, darling,' she heard him say before she lapsed into unconsciousness. 'Don't want you going AWOL again.'

Chapter Fifteen

'Spoke to Inspector Laing this morning, boss,' McCann was saying. 'They found Grossman's RAV4 parked in a lane near a cluster of cottages south of Canonbie.'

She was seated together with Fulton and Hathaway at the latter's computer, and Knox had joined them after his conversation with Warburton.

Hathaway nodded towards the monitor. 'He also gave us a link to a twenty-four-hour petrol station's CCTV recordings. It's situated near the junction of the A7 and B6357.'

'What time did Grossman pass the final Traffic Scotland checkpoint on his way south?'

'1.35am on Saturday.'

'And how far from there to where the RAV4 was found?'

'The B7201?' Hathaway said. 'About three miles.'

'I imagine it would be fairly quiet at that time of morning,' Knox said. 'Did many vehicles pass in the opposite direction in the hour following?'

'Only seven,' Hathaway replied. 'Five lorries, a Land Rover, and a BMW M60.'

'Headed back up the A7?'

'All but the Land Rover. That turned off at the B6357.'

'The road to Newcastleton?'

'Yeah, boss. A lot of farmland and villages en route.' He pointed to the monitor. 'Want to see the tape?'

Knox nodded. 'Yeah, let's have a look.'

Hathaway clicked on a file and a view of the A7/B6357 junction filled the screen. The young detective scrolled through the recording until the time at the top right read "2.13am, Saturday 15 April, 2023".

'When I roll the tape from this point you'll see two vehicles,' Hathaway explained. 'A Scania artic, followed a few seconds later by the Land Rover.'

The camera gave a wide-angle view of the A7 from the entry point of the filling station forecourt. The filling station was situated on a slight bend, opposite the B6357 junction. Knox saw the tractor unit of an articulated lorry appear first, followed by its trailer; the vehicle continued past the filling station and headed north. Immediately afterwards, the Land Rover came into view and turned into the B6357.

Knox pointed to the 4x4 as it disappeared from view. 'Rewind the tape, Mark,' he said. 'There's a clear view through the windscreen before he completes the turn.'

Hathaway did so, and froze the recording at the point where the Land Rover drew level with the junction and the driver began turning into the minor road.

'There,' Knox said, pointing to the screen.

'Looks like the ID shot we have on file,' McCann said. 'His face is a bit obscured by the cap he's wearing.'

'Where's Olivia, though?' Fulton asked.

'In the back, most likely,' Knox said. 'Didn't want to chance any local clocking her. He knew she'd be the subject of a missing persons bulletin.'

Hathaway nodded towards the image. 'Registration number's been obscured, too,' he said, peering closer and inspecting the registration plate. 'What's that, a clump of mud?'

'Aye,' Fulton said. 'Clever bugger. He probably checked out the filling station at some point on his travels, saw the CCTV.'

Hathaway pointed to the Land Rover. 'What colour would you say it is?'

'Hard to say with the filling station's tungsten lighting,' Knox replied. 'Grey, maybe. Or blue?'

McCann nodded. 'Blue, I think.'

Knox dipped his head towards the screen. 'Okay, Mark,' he said. Nothing else to be gleaned from that – you can switch it off.' Then to McCann, he added, 'Did Laing say anything about checking it out?'

'Yes, boss,' McCann replied. 'He's got uniform working along the route, showing locals Grossman's photograph. He's going to ask estate agents, too. See if anyone's recently bought property in the area. Promised to get back to me the moment he finds anything.'

McCann had just finished speaking when her iPhone rang. She took the mobile from her desk and glanced at the screen. 'Well, talk of the devil,' she said, and activated the device's speakerphone, placing it back on her desk.

'Hello?' she said.

'DS McCann?' a man replied. 'Dave Laing, Hawick Police. Calling you back about Ms Ledbetter?'

'Yes, sir,' McCann said.

'So far my lads have drawn a blank on estate agents. Not much joy with locals, either. There is something, however.'

'Yes, sir?' McCann replied. 'Please, carry on.'

'A local garage foreman here in Hawick called John Coulter phoned the office and spoke to one of my sergeants – Davie Wood – after a customer came into his garage to have a slow puncture fixed on his Ferrari Roma. The man said he would have done it himself except he'd forgotten his jack.

'He told Coulter he'd stopped near Newcastleton and asked a local, who apparently gave him a right earful.

Coulter said the man in question warned the Ferrari Roma owner he was on private land. The motorist told Coulter the man was with a girl who appeared distressed. He had a firm grip on the girl's arm, but let her go when he began getting hot under the collar, and the young woman made a run for it.'

'Where did this happen?' McCann asked.

'That's just it,' Laing replied. 'He told Coulter he wasn't sure. He came off the B6357 to do a bit of sightseeing near Newcastleton. Drove a few miles and discovered he had a slow puncture, which is when he had his encounter with the man and the girl. He came back onto the B6357 again and headed for Hawick.'

'The Ferrari Roma owner,' McCann said. 'He's still in Hawick?'

'Afraid not,' Laing replied. 'Sergeant Wood asked Coulter, who told him the man received a call on his mobile while the puncture was being fixed. He was needed urgently at his office in Edinburgh. Left immediately afterward.'

'Mr Coulter didn't get his address?'

'No.'

'The Ferrari Roma's registration number?

'No, I don't think so.'

'How did he pay Coulter?'

'It was a cash transaction so we won't be able to trace him via credit or debit card, either.'

Knox pointed to the phone and gestured that he wanted to speak to Laing.

'Inspector Laing,' McCann said, 'I've got you on speakerphone and my boss has been following the conversation. He'd like a word.'

'Ask him to go ahead,' Laing replied.

'This is DI Jack Knox, Inspector Laing,' Knox said. 'We're currently dealing with two cases here – the other's a multiple homicide. I think we're near a resolution with the latter, and I'd prefer to remain in Edinburgh until it's cleared up. In the meantime, DS McCann's been assigned to Olivia Ledbetter's abduction. I'd like her to go down to Hawick and lead the inquiry meantime – is that okay with you?'

'Of course, Detective Inspector,' Laing said. 'I'll offer her every assistance.'

Knox checked his watch. 'Thanks,' he replied. 'She'll be with you in a couple of hours.'

As McCann ended the call, Knox said, 'You don't mind, Arlene? I promised Warburton we'd get it dealt with ASAP; he's had HQ on his back. I'll get admin to arrange expenses for you and Mark. The two of you will probably have to stay overnight.'

'No problem, boss,' McCann replied. 'The change of air will do us a power of good.'

* * *

When Olivia came to, she found it almost impossible to move her arms. She glanced over her shoulder and saw her wrists had been tied to the bedposts with some kind of nylon rope.

But there was something else, too: when she moved, she felt a twinge at the back of her left hand. She turned and saw a needle had been inserted into a vein, from which a small plastic tube protruded.

At that moment, the bedroom door opened and Grossman entered. 'Ah, back with us again, darling?' he said condescendingly. 'Wondering why your arms are bound to the bedposts?' A pause. 'Simple, really. To keep you as immobile as possible, and let me keep a close eye on you.'

Olivia glanced at the back of her hand. 'But why have you–'

'Stuck a needle into your vein?' Grossman interrupted. He pointed to her hand. 'The tube is called a cannula. It enables me to administer drugs directly into your veins; they take effect more quickly.'

He went to the dressing table and Olivia saw the bag he'd put there on Saturday morning. Grossman opened it, took out a small bottle, placed it on the table, then extracted a small ampule, and stood it alongside.

He pointed to the container. 'This is ketamine, Olivia. An anaesthetic drug which I've used twice now.' He indicated the ropes binding her arms to the bedposts. 'And these,' he continued, 'would have been unnecessary if you'd continued to behave yourself.

'However, taking to your heels in full view of a stranger has put me in a precarious position. There's a strong possibility it will have alerted suspicions. No doubt resulting in a visit from the police in the very near future.'

'Then why—' Olivia began to say.

Grossman cut in. 'I hadn't finished,' he said and pointed to the ketamine. 'That will remain on the bedside table for just such an event. I'm sorry, Olivia, but you leave me no choice.'

'You really think they won't find me?' Olivia said.

'I honestly don't know,' Grossman replied. 'What I do know, however, is that I can't imagine going on without you.'

Olivia heard a catch in his throat, and was surprised to see tears in his eyes.

'Look, Clive,' she said. 'You have to accept those feelings are just not reciprocated.' She nodded to the restraints on her hands. 'Please, you have to let me go before you get into more serious trouble.' She paused. 'You know they'll find me. It's just a matter of time.'

'If that looks likely, Olivia, I will release you, I promise,' Grossman said ominously. 'And myself shortly afterwards,' he added.

Then he took the bottle from the dressing table and held it up. 'You see, Olivia, this is pentobarbital. Sleep follows thirty seconds after 10ml is injected. Thirty minutes later, the heart ceases to beat.' A pause. 'So, darling, we *will* be together… always.'

* * *

Grossman closed the bedroom door and walked back to the sitting room. His mobile rang. He glanced at the screen, saw who the caller was, and pressed *accept*.

'Hello, Archie,' he said. 'Where are you now?'

'I followed the A7 as you said, Mr Grossman. I'm passing through a place called Ashkirk.'

'Good,' Grossman said. 'Carry on four or five miles and you'll be in Hawick. Drive to the foot of the High Street, and you'll see Newcastleton signposted. It's the B6357.'

'I suppose it'd have been easier if I'd had sat nav,' the caller said. 'Driven forty years without it, though. Can't see me changing now.'

'Don't worry, it'll only take thirty minutes from Hawick. Ring me again when you're nearer. I'll wait for you at a place called the Olive Tree on the main street. You can follow my Land Rover to the house from there.'

'Ta, Mr Grossman.'

Grossman heard the man clear his throat.

'You did say a grand, didn't you?'

'Yes, Archie, £1,000: twenty fifty-pound notes. I have them in an envelope waiting for you.'

'And all I have to do is act like I own the place, do as you say, and I'm done?'

'Just like we discussed, Archie. Piece of cake, nothing to worry about.'

'Appreciate it, Mr Grossman, thanks. See you when I get there.'

Chapter Sixteen

An hour after McCann and Hathaway had departed for
Hawick, Knox was in the office with Fulton when he
received a call from Murray. He activated the device's
speakerphone and tapped *accept*.

'The results of the forensics, Jack,' Murray said.
'They're in.'

'From Balmoral Place?' Knox replied.

'And Spylaw Road. We got a result on DNA and Liz
identified the boot prints found on the floor in both
properties.'

'Whose DNA?'

'Curious thing', Murray replied. 'We ran it through the
database and it flashed up a fifty per cent match with the
sample file for Norman McVey.'

'Fifty per cent,' Knox said. 'What does that mean?'

'Familial DNA,' Murray said. 'It's almost certain McVey
and the killer are related.'

'You said Liz found a match with the prints on the
floor?'

'Yeah. Perfect match with the soles of a brand of boots
manufactured by a Czech company called Motonost. They
specialise in motorcycle gear.'

Knox and Fulton exchanged glances, then Knox said, 'I think we'll get a hundred per cent match on DNA from McVey's son, Ronald. How quickly can you get me the results?'

'Get a specimen of his blood up to Howdenhall and I'll endeavour to get it done today.' There was a pause while Murray checked the time. 'It's just after three now. Say around six, if I get the sample in the next hour?'

'Thanks, Ed. I'll get it to you ASAP,' Knox said. 'And thanks for the update.'

Knox ended the call and turned to Fulton. 'Get onto Haddington Police; have them arrest Ronald McVey and bring him in, Bill,' he said. 'I'll arrange for the duty medic to take a sample of blood when he gets here.'

* * *

'For the tape, there are four of us in the room,' Knox was saying into a NEAL recording machine. 'Ronald McVey and his legal representative, Mr Tristram Brandon. Also present are myself, Detective Inspector Knox, and my colleague, Detective Sergeant Fulton.'

The detectives were back in Interview Room 2, and Knox and Fulton were seated at a table opposite McVey and Brandon. A doctor had taken a blood sample when McVey arrived, which had been rushed to Howdenhall for testing.

'Mr McVey,' Knox continued, 'DNA found at the scene of a triple homicide which took place in Spylaw Road on Monday 17 April, and another at 46 Balmoral Place on Tuesday 18 April, was found to have a fifty per cent match to that of your father, Norman McVey – a reliable indicator of familial DNA.

'A blood sample taken on your arrival is currently being tested, and I'm sure it will provide a one hundred-per-cent match. In addition, prints found at both scenes match the soles of a pair of boots made in the Czech Republic, which you possess. Would you care to comment?'

'Pretty damning evidence,' McVey said.

'Pardon?' Knox replied.

'I said the evidence you have is conclusive, so there's no point in me protesting my innocence. I–'

'I advise you to say nothing more at the moment, Mr McVey,' Brandon interrupted. 'No charge has yet been made. Anything you say might be construed as incriminating.'

McVey gave the lawyer a dismissive wave. 'It's okay,' he said. 'No point in denying it.'

'You admit your guilt?' Knox said. 'You shot William Copeley, Thomas Reilly and Robert Scott at 101 Spylaw Road, and Hugh Leckie at 46 Balmoral Place?'

'Why should I say otherwise?' McVey replied. 'At this moment, cops are trashing my room at my dad's place. Bound to discover the pistol. A ballistics check will find it was bullets from the Beretta that put an end to the scum. And before long you'll have DNA results… so why lie?'

'Just to confirm,' Knox said. 'You admit to killing all four men?'

'Yes.'

'A moment ago you called them scum,' Knox said. 'Why?'

'You visited my dad,' McVey replied. 'You recall him saying my mum took ill in 2001?'

'Yes,' Knox replied.

'I was just a kid at the time; seven,' McVey continued. 'I remember she was in terrible pain. She knew she'd have to go to hospital, and was worried about who'd look after me, Dad being inside and all.'

'Your father told us she got in touch with Hugh Leckie's wife.'

'Aye, Joan,' McVey said. 'She was too good for Leckie; died a couple of years later, in 2003.' He paused, then went on. 'Anyway, Joan arrived, waited with my mum until the ambulance came, then we drove to their place in Gorebridge. I remember her making a meal; sitting down at the table with her and Leckie, who hadn't been at home when we first got there. He tousled my hair, made a fuss of me, and seemed quite likeable… at first.

'Joan worked as a supervisor at a knitwear firm in Peebles and was on a late shift that week. She kissed my cheek when she left, said I could stay up, watch telly, that Leckie would put me to bed, that she'd see me in the morning.

'About an hour later, three men arrived. They acted friendly, too. After a while, Leckie said, "Come on, Ronnie, time for bed."

'He took me through to the bedroom, undressed me, then I realised something was wrong. He began touching me…' McVey's hands tensed into fists, and his jaw clenched. 'And then–'

'He assaulted you?' Knox asked.

McVey nodded. He said nothing for a few moments, and then continued, 'But that wasn't the end of it. Soon after he left the room, he returned with Copeley, Reilly and Scott. "These nice men are going to tuck you in, Ronnie," he said. I remember being terrified and in pain, wondering what the hell was going on. One after the other, the bastards kept up the abuse until… I don't know, it must have been an hour but it seemed like eternity. They buggered off, leaving me clutching pillows, crying my eyes out.'

'You said nothing to Joan, Mrs Leckie?' Fulton asked.

McVey shook his head. 'I must've been drifting off. Leckie came back, left a box of Smarties and bottle of Coke. "You're not to tell anyone, Ronnie, understand?" he warned me. "Not Joan, not your mum and dad, nobody. Bad things will happen if you do. You don't want bad things to happen, do you, Ronnie?" I agreed I didn't, but he made me promise.'

'How long were you with the Leckies?' Knox asked.

'Seven days,' McVey replied. 'Till Mum had her operation and got out of hospital.'

'The abuse,' Knox said. 'It happened again?'

'Yeah, later in the week.'

'Leckie and the same three men?'

'Yeah.'

'You never mentioned it to anyone?'

'Nope,' McVey said. 'I was frightened at what Leckie had said. That bad things would happen.' A pause. 'A bit ashamed, too, as if for some reason I was to blame.'

'You never considered reporting them to us?' Knox said. 'Later, I mean.'

McVey nodded. 'A few times, yes. But as you say, I only *considered* it. I was worried about Mum and Dad, how it would affect them. It'd taken a long time for my mother to recover from her illness, I realised she'd blame herself – having been the one who asked Joan to look after me.

'Of course it had nothing to do with her or Joan, and everything to do with Leckie. But that wasn't how my mother would see it. It would have burdened her conscience, hampered her recovery. I decided to keep schtum.'

'What about your dad?' Knox said. 'Did you ever think of confiding in him?'

'Any number of times,' McVey replied. 'I decided not to for pretty much the same reason. In Dad's case, because he'd most likely kill Leckie and his three mates, which would have meant life for him, and would've devastated my mother.' McVey said nothing more for a moment, then added, 'I did come close to telling him when I was in my late teens, but after his accident at the wire works, I couldn't bring myself to.'

McVey paused for several seconds, then continued. 'I suffered nightmares right into my early twenties. Every one of them reliving what happened in Gorebridge. It affected my personality; I couldn't make friends or have lasting relationships with women. I took offence at the slightest thing.'

'Your dad told us you were engaged to a girl?' Fulton said.

'Yeah, Lorna,' McVey said. 'I didn't want to tell him, but we split up. For the reasons I just mentioned – she couldn't stand my moods.

'We were in High Street and ran into a group of kids playing kick-about football. One laddie – must've been about seven or eight – headed the ball and it hit Lorna's leg. I threw it back, told him to be more careful.

'Lorna smiled and said, "Suffer the little children". I don't know where it came from, but I suddenly saw red. "What do you know about children suffering?" I snapped at her. It started an argument that quickly became heated, then she broke down crying. Said she didn't want to see me again, and stormed off.'

'Which was when you decided to take revenge?'

McVey studied Knox for a long moment. 'I don't know much about psychology but, yeah, I reckon that was the catalyst. I'd bottled up my anger for more than twenty years. My moods were the result of the trauma I'd suffered. Losing Lorna was the last straw.'

'Where did you get the Beretta?' Knox asked.

'In Prague.'

'The Czech Republic?' Knox said. 'How did that come about?'

'Since 2016 I've been a self-employed courier driver; I own a Transit cargo van. Until Brexit took us out of the EU, most of my work came from firms buying machine parts in mainland Europe. One of my biggest contracts was with a company supplying parts to the car industry. The parts are manufactured near Prague, which meant I had to travel to the Czech Republic every week and spend a couple of nights there.

'I got friendly with a couple of lads at the Czech factory who were into pistol shooting. They invited me to their club, and over time I became quite an expert. One of the members sold me the Beretta, which I smuggled into the UK under one of the Transit's floor panels.'

'You brought the ammunition in the same way?'

'Yeah.'

'Did you buy the gun with the intention of killing Leckie and the others?' asked Knox.

McVey shook his head. 'Not really. The idea must have been in the back of my mind, but at the time, no, I hadn't consciously thought about it.'

'After your break-up with Lorna,' Knox said, 'and your decision to exact revenge, how did you discover where Leckie and the others would be?'

'Spylaw Road, you mean?'

'Yes.'

'My dad kept up with what Leckie was up to through the grapevine. I recalled him saying Leckie's latest project was a big house in Merchiston, which he intended turning into flats.

'After I broke up with Lorna, I went to Spylaw Road on my motorbike and kept watch on the house. The first couple of times I saw nobody. Then the third time, a Monday, I got lucky. Saw Leckie arrive in his Mercedes; Copeley, Reilly and Scott were with him. This would be late February, early March, and it was dark. I waited a while, went up to the front door, listened, and heard faint voices coming from the upper floor. I tried the door, and found it was open.

'I went inside, stood in the hallway, and listened again. They were in a room upstairs, playing cards. I guessed it must be a regular event, so I left and returned the following week and the week after, just to make sure.'

'All your ducks in a row; same place, same time?' Fulton said.

McVey shrugged, but said nothing.

'Except last Monday Leckie wasn't there?' Knox said.

'No, he wasn't,' McVey replied. 'I guessed he'd gone to ground, so I kept watch on his office. Easy enough to find

– it's in the phone book. Saw the young lad leave on his moped and followed him to Stockbridge.'

Knox nodded. 'I'm about to formally charge you, Ronald,' he said. 'But, before I do, I want to say that when your case comes to court, it's my hope that the circumstances will result in a lighter sentence.'

Chapter Seventeen

'Have trouble finding us?' Inspector Dave Laing was saying. He, McCann and Hathaway were seated in his office in Hawick Police Station and the Edinburgh detectives had only recently arrived.

McCann gave a little grin and nodded to Hathaway. 'Mark almost turned into the fire station by mistake, but no, sir, we followed the sat nav.'

'Ah,' Laing said. 'He's not the first to make that mistake, turning right instead of left. The buildings do look similar.' Laing paused and glanced at his notes. 'Okay, let me bring you up to date from where we were when I spoke to Inspector Knox.

'We decided to leave house-to-house inquiries until tomorrow, so we can give the Newcastleton area blanket coverage. We'll cast the net a bit wider, too; canvass businesses and show Grossman's photograph in Canonbie, Langholm, and here in Hawick.'

McCann gave a nod of acknowledgement, and checked her watch; it was approaching 5pm. 'The garage where the foreman John Coulter works, sir,' she said, 'is it still open?'

'Aye,' Laing replied. 'J&M Motors. Dovecote Street, just off the High Street. Closes at six.'

'I'd like to have another word with Mr Coulter, sir, if you don't mind.'

'Not at all, that's a good idea,' Laing replied. 'Might be something we missed.'

Laing paused and added, 'Oh, by the way, Inspector Knox asked me to arrange accommodation for yourself and DC Hathaway. I've booked a couple of rooms at The Hawick Hotel in the High Street. Just around the corner from J&M Motors.'

'Thank you, sir,' McCann said. 'I'd also like us to take part in the house-to-house inquiries in Newcastleton.'

'Of course,' Laing said. 'I've arranged for myself and six PCs to leave the station at 8am. You'll join us?'

'Yes, sir. We'll be here at eight.'

* * *

J&M Motors was situated at the far end of Dovecote Street, which, as Laing had said, led off the northern end of Hawick's High Street. The street was long and narrow, and Hathaway had to park his Astra part-way onto the pavement to allow room for other vehicles.

The detectives entered the garage and saw a teenager in overalls rolling a trolley jack under an old Austin Cambridge. He turned and eyed the detectives with interest. 'Yeah?' he said.

'We're looking for a Mr John Coulter,' McCann said. 'I believe he's the foreman?'

The teenager nodded, turned to face a portacabin at the other end of the premises, and cupped a hand to his mouth. 'Johnnie,' he called out. 'Somebody here to see you!'

Moments later, a small man in his early sixties opened the portacabin door and walked over. He looked beyond the detectives and saw the Astra parked near the entrance. 'We're almost closed for the day, I'm afraid,' he said. 'If it's a service or repair, it'll have to wait till tomorrow.'

McCann showed him her warrant card. 'The car's okay,' she said. 'You're Mr Coulter?'

The man nodded. 'Aye, I am,' he replied. 'What's the problem?'

'We're investigating the disappearance of a young girl, Olivia Ledbetter. You spoke to Sergeant Wood at Hawick Police earlier today concerning a man driving a Ferrari Roma?'

'Aye, that's right,' Coulter said. 'He had a slow puncture and no jack.' Coulter pointed towards the teenager, who had positioned the trolley jack beneath the Cambridge and was levering it off the floor. 'Malkie put on his spare. I spoke to the guy while the job was being done.'

'We'd like to go over exactly what he told you,' McCann explained. 'From the time he came in until he left.'

Coulter took an oily rag from his overall pocket and began wiping his hands. 'Well,' he said, 'it's like I told the sergeant. For some reason he'd mislaid his jack. Told me he drove with a partly inflated tyre all the way from Newcastleton. By the time he got here, it was almost on its rims.'

'What time was this? McCann asked.

'Around twelve.'

'Okay,' McCann said. 'Carry on.'

'Well, like I say, I asked Malkie to put on the spare. Told the man there was no use trying to patch up the tyre that came off – the rubber walls were finished, what with him running it flat and all.' Coulter adjusted a pair of spectacles on his nose. 'I offered to put on a new one. I think he was about to agree, then his mobile rang. He told me it was his secretary, that he was wanted in his office. Said he'd take a chance and run on the spare.'

'What did he tell you about the girl?' McCann asked.

'Oh, aye,' Coulter said. 'We got chatting while Malkie was changing the tyre. He told me he'd driven up from Carlisle, where he'd been on business for a couple of days.

Driving through Longtown he saw a sign for Newcastleton. He told me he'd visited the town as a kid and decided to do a bit of sightseeing.'

'But he came off the B6357?'

'Aye, took the single-track road from Newcastleton to Langholm. Nice drive, particularly in an open top like a Ferrari.'

'Which was when he discovered he had a puncture?'

'Yeah, after only a few miles. He stopped, and discovered his jack was missing. Told me he was passing a cottage set back off the road. Slowed with the intention of asking whoever owned it if they had one he could borrow. It was then he saw the man and the girl.'

'Near the cottage?' McCann asked.

'Open space beyond, from what I understand.'

'Go on.'

'He approached the man, asked if he could borrow a jack. The guy blew up at him, told him it was private property and asked him to leave.'

'The girl,' McCann said. 'She was by his side?'

'Apparently,' Coulter replied. The Ferrari chap said the man was holding the girl by the wrist. He became distracted and she broke free, began running towards some woods.'

'And the man gave chase?' Hathaway said.

'My customer didn't say. He told me he left the property and went back to his car. Decided the single-track road might be a bit risky with the soft tyre. Drove back to the B6357 and headed for Hawick.'

McCann nodded. 'Sergeant Wood said you told him the motorist paid cash?'

'Aye, came to £67.50.'

'You gave him a receipt?'

Coulter shook his head. 'He told me not to bother. This was only a few minutes after he'd taken the call on his mobile. Told me he'd have to skedaddle.'

'So, no address…'

'Sorry, no.'

'Registration number?'

'No,' Coulter said. 'The Ferrari was red, though.'

McCann gestured towards the teenager, who'd disappeared under the Austin on a dolly; only his legs were visible. 'What about your employee?' she said. 'He fixed the puncture?'

'Yeah, you're right,' Coulter replied, 'I'll ask him.' The foreman walked the short distance to the car. 'Malkie?' he said.

'Aye?' the young man replied.

'Come out from under there a minute, will you, son? These people are detectives. They'd like to ask you about the Ferrari you worked on earlier.'

Malkie slid from beneath the car and got to his feet. 'Aye, what about it?'

'We were asking about the Ferrari driver,' McCann said. 'Mr Coulter told us he didn't want a receipt and left in a bit of a hurry. You didn't happen to get the registration number, did you?'

'Aye, I did,' Malkie said. 'Couldn't miss it. TOM 1H.'

* * *

McCann's inquiry to Police Scotland's Internal Communications Centre was answered at 7.41pm. She and Hathaway had booked into The Hawick Hotel, been allocated their rooms and had dinner, and were seated in a small lounge at the front, which was empty save for an elderly man reading *The Telegraph*.

The detectives had just taken their place near the window when the call came in. 'Hello?' McCann answered.

'Detective Sergeant McCann?' A woman's voice said.

'Speaking.'

'We received a reply to your request to identify the registered keeper of plate number TOM 1H, and conduct a search of the owner's details?'

'Yes,' McCann replied.

'The vehicle is registered to a Thomas McClure, 25 Heriot Mews, Edinburgh. We found three telephone numbers. The first at the office address of his business, McLure Investment and Hedge Fund Management, 351 Queen Street, Edinburgh. The second at his home address in Heriot Mews, and the third, a mobile number. Would you like me to text these to you?'

'I'd appreciate if you would, thanks,' McCann replied.

She ended the call. Then, moments later, the elderly man lowered his newspaper and gave a disapproving look as her iPhone beeped loudly.

McCann indicated the device and addressed Hathaway. 'The ICC,' she said quietly. 'The Ferrari's owned by a man called Thomas McClure. Three numbers: his office, home phone, and mobile.'

Hathaway checked his watch. 'Not likely to be in his office at this time.'

'You never know,' McCann countered.

At that moment the old man gave a grunt, folded his newspaper, stood up and walked out.

'Good,' McCann said, nodding to her mobile. 'I'll put it on speakerphone. We can both listen.'

She found McClure's office number, pressed *call*, and a female voice replied after three rings. 'Hello, McClure Investments.'

'Hello,' McCann said. 'Can I speak to Mr Thomas McClure, please?'

'May I ask who's calling?'

'Detective Sergeant McCann, Edinburgh Police.'

A pause, then, 'Hold on, please.'

Some moments passed, then the detectives heard a male voice. 'Hello, McClure.'

'Good evening, sir,' McCann said. 'Sorry to call so late, but we're investigating the disappearance of a young woman, Olivia Ledbetter. We interviewed Mr Coulter, the foreman at J&M Motors in Hawick, who told us you said you may have seen her today?'

'Ah, yes. When my Ferrari developed a puncture.'

'It happened near Newcastleton, I believe?'

'Yes, I'd driven up from a business meeting in Carlisle. Decided to leave the A7 and go via Newcastleton. I had an aunt who had a cottage at North Liddle Street, next to Liddel Water. Spent some summers there as a boy.'

'You went off the B-road at some point?' McCann said.

'Yes, sorry. I stopped, had a cup of coffee at the Olive Tree café, then remembered a single-track road leading to Langholm that my brother and I used to trek when staying with my aunt – part-way, anyway, not the entire route. I was in no particular hurry at that point.'

'What time would this be?'

'Around 10am, I think.'

'Okay,' McCann replied. 'Carry on.'

'I must have covered three or four miles before I felt the rear end begin to drift. I stopped and saw the puncture. Wasn't completely flat, but close. I opened the boot, discovered the jack was missing, then remembered I'd taken it out in my garage. I'd heard a rattle a day or two earlier, and was checking the spare wheel retainers were secure. Like an idiot, I forgot to put it back.'

'When you stopped, you saw the cottage?' McCann asked.

'No, it was half a mile farther on.'

'Can you describe what it looked like?'

'Yes,' McClure replied. 'Located back off the road; positioned at a slight angle, and accessed by a long gravel driveway. Fairly large. White or cream painted, if I remember correctly.'

'I see,' McCann said. 'Carry on.'

'I stopped again with the intention of approaching the entrance, then heard voices.' McClure continued. 'Male and female, coming from the other side of the cottage. I walked a short distance, saw the rear backed onto a wide meadow, fenced at either side, with a thickly wooded area opposite.'

'Which is when you saw the couple?'

'Yes.'

'They were near the cottage?'

'No, a third of the way between the cottage and the woods.'

'Okay,' McCann said. 'Carry on.'

'I checked if there was a way to get closer,' McClure said. 'Between me and the fence was a small stream; a rivulet really, narrower in some places than others. I found a spot where it was little more than a foot wide, crossed easily and found a gap in the fence and ducked through.'

'The man saw you approach?' McCann asked.

'Only when I was fifty yards away.'

'How did they appear?'

'I'm not sure I know what you mean.'

'Did the situation seem normal, as if they were taking a walk, or were they arguing? Did the woman act as if she was under duress?'

'Oh, I see,' McClure said. 'Sorry. Yes, that's the strange thing. They did act normally… at first. Then a moment or so later, I saw the man turn on the girl, as if she'd said something to upset him. He grabbed her by the wrist and turned to face the cottage. This happened almost at the same time as I called out to ask if he could help me.'

'How did he react?'

'He appeared shocked,' McClure said. 'Then became incensed. Said I'd no right to be on his property, that it was private land. I tried to explain that I only wanted to borrow a jack, but he was having none of it. Told me to bugger off.'

'He let go of the girl?'

'Only when he pointed towards me to emphasise his point. She took to her heels and ran for the woods.'

'He ran after her?'

'I didn't see him do so,' McClure said. 'He appeared rooted to the spot – glancing first at me, then her. I think he shouted for her to stop, but I didn't hang around. I retraced my steps and went back to the car. I'm afraid I didn't deem it all that important at the time. A young couple having some sort of row, perhaps.'

'Had you seen television bulletins regarding the missing girl, Olivia Ledbetter?' McCann asked.

'Yes, at my hotel in Carlisle,' McClure said. 'But at the time I failed to make the connection.' He paused. 'I was preoccupied with the tyre and it was only when I arrived in Hawick that I gave it any thought. I mentioned it to the foreman when I had my puncture fixed. Then my secretary called to say I was needed at the office. I left it with the man at the garage, who promised to report it to the local police.'

'Thank you, Mr McClure,' McCann said. 'That's been helpful. You'll be in Edinburgh if we need to verify anything in the next day or two?'

'Yes, either here at my office or at home. You have my numbers?'

'Yes, sir, we do.'

Chapter Eighteen

Warburton exited his office and beckoned to Knox. 'Can I have a word, Jack?' he said.

A few moments later Knox was seated opposite his boss, who gestured to a phone on his desk. 'It's the ACC,' he said. 'Been breathing down my neck. Not happy with the pace of our inquiries into the abduction of the Ledbetter girl.'

'I don't see why,' Knox said. 'We know Grossman's likely to be in the Newcastleton area. Laing will commence a house-to-house first thing in the morning. DS McCann and DC Hathaway are there, too. It can only be a matter of time.'

'You've hit the nail on the head, Jack – time. I've a feeling Marcus Ledbetter thinks it's taking too long.'

'Well, as I said–'

'I know, Jack, I know,' Warburton interrupted. 'You're doing everything possible in the circumstances.' The DCI checked his watch again. 'Almost five-thirty,' he said. 'Head office informed me the ACC would ring at half past five. Apparently he wants to speak to you, too.'

Knox made a face. 'Olivia's father must be rattling their chains.'

Warburton harrumphed. 'You know what they say, Jack. A squeaky door gets the most oil.' A pause. 'I gather Mr Ledbetter gave you a hard time?'

'A bit,' Knox said. 'Not without justification, though. Considering what we've learned of Grossman.'

A shrill ring jolted Warburton, who lifted the telephone handset and said, 'Hello?'

Knox saw his boss take on a chastened expression.

'Yes, sir.' A moment or two, then, 'Yes sir… but–' A few moments later, Warburton covered the mouthpiece and passed the handset to Knox. 'The ACC,' he said. 'Wants a word.'

'Hello, sir,' Knox said. 'DI Knox speaking.'

'Knox,' the voice said. 'ACC Alan Moodie. You've no doubt gathered I'm calling about Olivia Ledbetter's abduction. Five days now and still no result. The media is on our backs 24/7. The Scottish Police Authority minister at Holyrood is asking for an update every five minutes – and I've nothing to tell either. Why the hell is it taking so long?'

'Grossman set up the abduction very carefully, sir, built in a few red herrings.'

'Pardon?'

Knox explained the different steps the team had gone through to identify Grossman's car and their current lead following the information they'd received from the garage in Hawick.

Moodie was not best pleased but had to agree that it sounded like they were doing all they could.

'I understand the multiple murders case you were investigating reached a conclusion?' he said.

'Yes, sir, the perpetrator, Ronald McVey, has been charged.'

'Which leaves you free to join McCann?'

'Yes, sir. She'll be phoning me with an update later this evening. I intend driving to Newcastleton first thing in the morning.'

'Good,' Moodie replied. 'Okay, Knox, I'll leave it with you. Get that bugger Grossman. I want to see Ms Ledbetter found by tomorrow.'

* * *

Archie Gibson awoke a little after 7am, and at first failed to recognise his surroundings. Then he remembered: Clive Grossman had met him at a café in Newcastleton's main street and he'd followed him to the cottage. They'd had dinner and a few beers, discussed the deal, then Grossman had shown him to a small bedroom situated at the back of the house.

When they arrived, Grossman had garaged his Land Rover, then asked Archie to park his Mondeo on the driveway close to the gate. He'd then obscured the view by moving two large wheeled wooden planters to hide the car's number plates.

After the meal, Grossman had gone over his plan. 'Your name is Ralph Bellamy,' he'd told Archie. 'The man who owned the cottage before I bought it. Like I say, I never changed the deeds. If the police check the property register, their suspicions won't be aroused.'

Quite a clever lad, Clive, Archie thought. Mindful of every detail.

He cast his mind back to when they first met. It had been late January, and he'd been sitting on his favourite stool at Middleton's Bar at the corner of Easter Road and Edina Street. Grossman came in and took the stool alongside, they got chatting, and Grossman had asked what he did for a living. Archie told him he was a painter and decorator.

'That's a coincidence,' Grossman said. 'I've just bought a flat in Elgin Terrace, a few minutes' walk from here. I'm looking for someone to help me do up the place. Would you be interested?'

Grossman was personable, had an easy way about him, and Archie felt he could trust the young man enough to take him into his confidence.

'I'm sixty-three, son,' he'd told Grossman. 'Spent most of my life in and out of prison. Housebreaking. Done with it now, though – getting too long in the tooth. I'm telling you this as it's likely you'll find out, anyway.' A pause. 'Might want to change your mind about offering me the job.'

'Not at all,' Grossman replied. 'We all make mistakes, myself included.' He'd smiled and added, 'When can you start?'

Archie had begun helping Grossman decorate his flat later that week, beginning first with the living room, then moving into the kitchen.

Grossman worked during the day, commuting via the Queensferry Crossing to the pharmaceutical firm in Fife, but he was always ready to roll up his sleeves and join Archie on his return.

On the Monday of the following week, Grossman was putting on a second coat of satin in the kitchen and Archie was painting a cupboard, when the young man had asked, 'Are you married, Archie?'

'Was,' Archie replied. 'We divorced fifteen years ago. She got fed up with me breaking my promises to go straight.'

'So, you live on your own?'

'No,' Archie replied. 'With my sister, Nan. My ex-wife was awarded the house in the settlement. Nan was kind enough to let me have her spare room.'

'Oh,' Grossman replied.

'What about you,' Archie had asked. 'Engaged? This is to be your place when you marry?'

Grossman shook his head. 'No, just a property I bought to use on a temporary basis.'

'You're seeing a girl, though?'

'Yes, Olivia. Met her at St Andrews, the university I attended until I graduated in November.'

'The relationship,' Archie asked. 'It's serious?'

'Oh, yes,' Grossman said. 'Very. I want her to be my wife.'

'When are you going to pop the question?'

Grossman had remained silent for a moment or two, then said, 'It's difficult. She returns my feelings and all that, but isn't sure she wants to settle down.'

'How old is she?' Archie asked.

'Twenty,' Grossman replied. 'Almost twenty-one.'

'What does she study at St Andrews?'

'Law.'

'Ah,' Archie said. 'She'd rather pursue a career?'

'She doesn't have to,' Grossman said. 'I inherited a large sum from an aunt. Enough to ensure we live comfortably for the rest of our lives.'

'Aye, well, Clive, you know what they say; money isn't everything.'

'What do you mean?'

'Maybe the lass values her independence,' Archie said, then laughed. 'Listen to me, giving advice. If I'd stuck to my trade instead of following a life of crime, it's probable that Kate – my ex-wife – and I would still be together.'

'I'm sure it isn't that she particularly wants a career,' Grossman said. 'She has feelings for me and wouldn't mind settling down, I'm positive of that. It's her father. Hot-shot lawyer. Prosecutes high-profile cases in London. He wants Olivia to follow in his footsteps.'

'You've met him?'

'No, but she's mentioned him on several occasions.'

'Maybe you should talk to him. Tell him you're financially secure, persuade him you've his daughter's interests at heart.'

'No,' Grossman said. 'There has to be another way. I'm confident I'll find it.'

The flat in Edina Street had been completely redecorated in just under three weeks, and on the last day Grossman handed Archie an envelope.

He riffled through a bundle of twenties and looked at Grossman in astonishment. 'There's £800 here,' he said. 'I was going to charge £450.'

'Worth it, Archie,' Grossman had said. 'You've done an excellent job.'

'Not on my own, though. You did a fair bit yourself.' Archie eyed the envelope and added, 'That's more than generous.'

'No problem, Archie,' Grossman replied. 'You never know, I might call on your services again sometime.'

'Any time, Clive,' Archie had replied. 'Any time.'

Which was what had happened. Archie advertised on cards in local shop windows and in the trades section of Gumtree, but over the last week things had been quiet. Then, just before lunchtime the day before, he received a call on his mobile.

He hadn't recognised the caller's number, and answered, 'Hello, Gibson Decorating Services, Archie Gibson speaking.'

'Hello, Archie? Clive Grossman. You helped decorate my flat at Edina Street back in January. Said if I had any other work I should give you a ring?'

'Aye, Clive,' Archie said. 'Of course. What's the job?'

'I've a bit of a problem. You recall me telling you I was seeing a girl I hoped to marry?'

'Aye, Clive, I do. She was thinking of following a career in law. You were confident you'd get her to change her mind?'

'Right, Archie. Well, the good news is I did. Got her to change her mind, I mean. Bought a lovely cottage down in the Borders. We've only just moved in.'

'Good for you, Clive,' Archie said. 'When did you get married?'

'We aren't married,' Grossman said. 'Not yet, anyway.'

'You said you had a problem?'

'Yes, her father. You may remember me telling you about him?'

'Aye. He wanted the girl to follow in his footsteps?'

'Exactly. Well, the thing is, he's a complete ogre. Had his daughter under his thumb since she was a child. To say she's terrified of him is to put it mildly. We acted against his wishes, and he reacted by creating a hullabaloo. Got the police involved; told them she was abducted.'

Archie thought for a moment. 'The girl on the telly – the one they say is missing,' he said. *That's* your fiancée?'

'Yes, Archie,' Grossman said. 'Olivia. We came down here to escape his clutches. Somewhere quiet and out of reach. Or so we believed.'

'Why don't you speak to him, tell him his daughter's with you of her own free will? Nothing he can do about it. He'll have to call off the cops.'

'I would, except her father's got her so cowed that she's suffered a nervous breakdown. I was hoping to see her return to normal before we took that step. Then today a chap trespassed on my property looking to borrow a jack. I got rid of him, but Olivia had a panic attack afterwards. She was worried the police would discover our whereabouts and alert her father.'

'Jeez,' Archie said. 'He must be a right bastard if he affects her in that way.'

'He is, Archie. Luckily I was able to give her a sedative to calm her down.'

'Poor lass,' Archie said. 'How can I help?'

'The police,' Grossman said. 'The chap I ordered off my property is bound to have recognised Olivia. Can't be long till they canvas the area and identify me as the man her father claims is an abductor. I was hoping you'd drive down and answer the door, tell them you own the property.'

'I dunno, Clive…'

'Nothing to worry about, Archie. The house isn't registered in my name yet. The former owner lost his wife a few months back. He leased it to me for a year with an option to buy. Went to live with his sister in Melrose. He's around your age. Suspicions wouldn't be raised if anyone checked the property register.' A pause. 'I'll pay a grand for your trouble, Archie, and I've a spare room you can stay in while you're here.'

'That's all you want?' Archie said. 'Me to pretend to be this other guy?'

'That's all, Archie. Like I say, I'll pay you a grand.'

'Okay, I'll do it. Where in the Borders are you?'

'Make for Newcastleton, near Hawick,' Grossman had replied. 'Give me a ring when you're near. We'll meet and you can follow me to the cottage.'

Chapter Nineteen

'A search of the property register for the nearest dwellings gives information for owners on the road between here and Langholm,' Inspector Laing was saying.

It was shortly before 9am, and his team of six constables were seated in the office of Newcastleton Police Station in Langholm Street. Also in the room were

McCann and Hathaway, who had met Laing and his men at Hawick and followed them to the town.

Laing pointed to a portly man in his early sixties seated nearby. 'This is Sergeant Duffy,' Laing said. 'Newcastleton Police. He conducted the search for us at short notice, and also gave me some pointers on local topography.' Laing nodded towards Duffy and added, 'He will continue with local business while we conduct the search for Grossman.'

Laing indicated the officers who'd accompanied him from Hawick. 'You men will form three teams of two and begin a house-to-house here in Newcastleton. Show photographs of Grossman and Olivia to locals and find out if anyone witnessed anything out of the ordinary. Grossman was last seen driving a blue Land Rover. Remember to mention that – it might jog someone's memory. Remember also to listen to your radios, and keep your vehicles handy. When Grossman's discovered I want every man to be ready to drop what he's doing and head for his location.'

His attention was caught by McCann, who had her hand raised. 'Yes, DS McCann?'

'The houses between here and Langholm, sir,' she said. 'I assume DC Hathaway and I will begin with them?'

Laing dipped his head in confirmation. 'Yes, I was coming to that. I gave Sergeant Duffy a précis of your conversation with McClure. He thinks the description could fit any one of three properties en route.' He turned to Duffy. 'Sergeant Duffy?'

The sergeant stood, and cleared his throat. 'Yes, the layout outlined by Mr McClure is similar to that of a couple of cottages and a B&B on the first section of the road. All three sit at a slight angle to the tarmac and have a patch of land and a wooded area nearby.'

'What about a stream?' McCann said. 'McClure told us there was one separating the meadow from the roadway.'

'There's a fair number of burns and runnels near all three,' Duffy said. 'Water off the hills.'

McCann nodded. 'The names on the register, Sergeant, could you let me have them, please?'

'Aye, sure,' Duffy said and consulted his notebook. 'We're in Langholm Street, which is the start of the Newcastleton-Langholm road. Continue on for a couple of miles and you'll come to the first, a cottage belonging to a Mr Mills. Only moved in last year, so I don't know him. The next is situated around four miles further on, after a series of bends. Owned by a chap called Bellamy, who lives on his own. Quiet lad; lost his wife last November. I haven't seen him since her funeral. A mile beyond that is the B&B, run by Charlie Taylor. He has a few outbuildings he rents to tourists, might be worth checking out.'

'Thank you,' McCann said. 'We will.'

Laing looked about the room and rubbed his hands together. 'Right, if there are no other questions, we can get going.'

'One thing I forgot to mention, sir,' McCann said.

'Yes, DS McCann?'

'My boss, DI Knox, gave me a ring last night. The other case we were on?'

'Uh-huh, he mentioned. A triple homicide?'

'Yes, sir,' McCann replied. 'It was solved yesterday; the killer charged.'

'So, Inspector Knox is on his way to join us?'

'Yes, sir. Rang me again just before we arrived. Should be here in an hour.'

'Good,' Laing said with a thin smile. 'The more the merrier.'

* * *

Archie Gibson found a toilet next to his bedroom. He emptied his bladder, washed his hands and face in a small hand basin, then took a comb from his shirt pocket and ran it through his hair.

He exited and saw Grossman standing at a corner of the hallway a short distance away.

'Morning, Archie,' his host said. 'Sleep well?'

'Aye, like a log, thanks,' Gibson replied, then, stroking the stubble on his chin, he added, 'Forgot to bring a razor, though.'

'I'd let you borrow mine,' Grossman said, 'but it's electric.'

'Ach, can't use those things; bring me out in blotches. Should be okay, Clive. I shaved yesterday.'

'I was on my way to ask if you'd like breakfast,' Grossman said. 'Got the Aga fired up, kettle on the boil.' A pause. 'Full Scottish?'

'Aye, I *am* a bit hungry.'

'Right, Archie, full Scottish it is,' Grossman said. 'Follow me.'

A short while later Gibson was tucking into a plate of bacon, eggs and sausage, accompanied by potato scones, grilled tomatoes and mushrooms.

In between mouthfuls he motioned to Grossman's plate. 'Scrambled eggs and toast, Clive,' he said. 'You're not hungry?'

'I always eat light in the morning,' Grossman replied.

Gibson nodded, swallowed, and took a swig of tea. 'How's the lass this morning?' he asked, returning his mug to the table.

Grossman shook his head. 'Olivia's still sedated. Awoke a couple of hours ago, around six. Had some cereal and a glass of milk, then fell asleep again.'

'She's okay, though?' Gibson said. 'Not ill, needing to see a doctor?'

'No, nothing like that,' Grossman replied. 'We spoke for a couple of hours after you went to bed. She was still worried about the likelihood of police calling this morning. Had to take another sedative to help her sleep.'

'Helluva thing,' Gibson said. 'Her father affecting her like that.'

'I know,' Grossman replied.

'You definitely think the police might pay a visit this morning?'

'Positive,' Grossman said. 'As a matter of fact, I saw the local plod patrolling in his Land Rover earlier. Checking in advance of a larger force from Hawick and Edinburgh, no doubt.'

Gibson put down his knife and fork and gave Grossman a worried look. 'When they get here, Clive,' he said. 'You're sure I'll pass muster?'

'Of course, Archie. Like I told you, you've nothing to concern yourself about. Bellamy was around your age, became a widower when his wife died last November. We covered all other details vis-a-vis the property and that sort of thing yesterday.'

'But what about this local cop?' Gibson said. 'He's bound to have known Bellamy.'

'He won't be involved,' Grossman replied. 'Except to brief the officers who'll conduct the inquiries. That's why they're calling on manpower from other forces – too much for one man to handle.'

'You're sure?'

'Of course, Archie,' Grossman said. 'Follow the script and you'll be okay.' He gestured to Gibson's plate. 'Now come on, stop worrying and finish your breakfast.'

* * *

Between Wednesday evening and Thursday morning, Olivia slipped in and out of consciousness. She was semi-awake for short periods, during which she was aware of Grossman standing by the bed, checking the cannula and loosening the nylon rope that bound her to the bedposts. She was glad of that, as her arms had begun to ache badly.

A couple of times she thought she heard voices, but most of the time she'd been in a drugged torpor and hadn't been sure it wasn't part of a dream.

Her eyes opened, and at that moment she did hear voices – clearly and distinctly. Grossman was talking to a man. She thought she heard him say something about breakfast, then he and the stranger must have moved into the kitchen, as she heard the sound of pans rattling about on the cooker.

The effort of concentrating suddenly made her feel woozy, then everything in the room faded, and once again she blacked out.

Olivia came to a second time as Grossman entered the room. He closed the door behind him, went to the dressing table, and picked up the hypodermic syringe.

He turned to face Olivia and saw she was conscious. 'Ah, sorry, darling,' he said quietly, 'didn't realise you were awake.'

'Someone's here,' Olivia said weakly. 'I heard you talking.'

'You did indeed,' Grossman said. 'A friend of mine.' A pause. 'You remember we spoke earlier about the likelihood of the police calling? Well, I've asked my friend to answer and pretend to be the man from whom I bought the property. This will, I hope, delay them discovering your whereabouts a little longer.' Grossman gestured towards the bottle of pentobarbital on the dresser. 'Give me time to think of an alternative to that.'

'Your friend,' Olivia said groggily. 'He knows I'm here against my will?'

'Let's just say he knows you're here,' Grossman replied. He tapped the syringe, pressed the plunger a little, and a narrow stream of ketamine spurted from the needle. 'Which I'll make sure he continues to think is voluntarily. So, time for another little shot. Sorry, darling. Just enough to keep you quiet until the police have been and my friend departs.'

* * *

'Hello, is that Detective Inspector Knox?'

The voice came over the Passat's speakers in response to Knox pressing the *accept* icon on his mobile on the dash.

The detective was passing through an area known as Caddroun View on his way to Newcastleton.

'Yes, DI Knox speaking.'

'Good morning, my name's Colin Medwin, manager of G&R Pharmaceuticals in Donibristle, Fife. I spoke to one of your officers, a DC Hathaway. I phoned your office and they gave me your number.'

'Yes, Mr Medwin, DC Hathaway mentioned it. He was told some of your drugs are missing. That it's possible your ex-employee, Clive Grossman, may have something to do with their disappearance.'

'Well, that's what I'm calling about, actually. I'm afraid there's been a bit of a mix-up.'

'Oh?'

'Yes. One of our warehousemen in the DDA store shelved a consignment in the wrong place.'

'Go on,' Knox said.

'Regarding the missing items,' Medwin said, 'I told DC Hathaway they were ketamine and pentobarbital, that was a mistake. Ketamine *is* one of the missing drugs, but the other isn't pentobarbital.'

'It isn't?' Knox said.

'No, it's phenobarbital. As I say, the delivery from our supplier was wrongly shelved in the storeroom. Our warehouseman misread the shipping label, I'm afraid.'

'DC Hathaway was told that pentobarbital is supplied to facilities in Switzerland, where it's used in euthanasia?'

'Yes, that's correct.'

'Grossman took phenobarbital in place of pentobarbital?'

'We think so, yes. We're still verifying our stock levels, but it looks like it may be the case. The bottles are very similar in appearance, the only difference is in the labelling.'

'Phenobarbital,' Knox said. 'What is it used for?'

'It's an anti-seizure medication,' Medwin replied. 'Prescribed mainly for epileptics. Also used to help patients in benzodiazepine and alcohol withdrawal.'

'So it's not dangerous?'

'Not unless taken in exceptionally large doses. In such cases the patient would require to be hospitalised immediately.'

Chapter Twenty

The first cottage McCann and Hathaway came to was, as Sergeant Duffy had said, set back off the road. But, other than that, bore no similarity to the property McClure had described. The harling on the walls was more yellow than white, and there was no meadow at the rear of the house, nor any wooded area nearby.

'McClure told me when the girl broke free she ran to some woods,' McCann said. 'The nearest trees are half a mile away.'

'And on the opposite side of the road,' Hathaway said.

'Yeah,' McCann said. 'And look at the paint on the exterior walls. McLure told me white or cream.'

The detectives exited the car. 'What did Duffy say the owner's name was?' McCann said.

Hathaway consulted his notebook. 'Mills,' he replied. 'David Mills.'

McCann unlatched a wooden gate and the detectives walked up a path to the door. Hathaway lifted an old-fashioned knocker, rapped three times, and almost immediately a dog began to bark.

'Sounds like a collie,' McCann said.

'No, a bit more deep-throated,' Hathaway countered. 'Like an Alsatian.'

A few moments later a woman in her late sixties opened the door a fraction and peered out. 'Yes?' she said.

The dog, which the detectives still couldn't see, continued barking at the other side of the door.

McCann held up her warrant card. 'Police,' she said, straining to make her voice heard. 'We're calling about a missing girl, Olivia Ledbetter. We've reason to believe she may be in the area and wondered if you'd seen anything.' She pointed towards where she imagined the dog to be. 'Would it be possible to have a word?'

'Oh, I see – right,' the woman said. 'Can you wait until I take Molly to the back? She's excited because she's about to go out with my husband. We're moving sheep to another field. I'll have to close the door a minute – you don't mind?'

'No,' McCann said, giving Hathaway a look of triumph. 'Not at all.'

The woman reappeared moments later, opened the door, and waved the detectives inside. 'The kitchen's straight along the hallway and to your right,' she said. 'My husband put Molly in the Land Rover. He's waiting in case you need to talk to us both.'

'Thank you,' McCann said. She and Hathaway entered the kitchen and were met by a ruddy-faced man wearing a boiler suit and Wellington boots.

'This is my husband, Davie,' Mrs Mills said.

Her husband nodded and indicated a couple of chairs positioned at a table. 'Please, take a seat,' he said. 'My wife says you're here in connection with the missing girl?'

'Yes,' McCann replied.

'She's here, in Newcastleton?'

'We've reason to think she might be,' McCann replied. 'Her abductor's a man in his mid-twenties, last seen driving a blue Land Rover. You don't happen to have seen either?'

Mr Mills shook his head. 'Practically the transport of choice in these parts,' he said. 'Land Rovers. Japanese four-wheel-drives, too, of course. Quite a few farms, and a lot of off-road work.' A pause. 'Can't say I've noticed any with a driver around that age, though. Most folk around here are getting on a bit.'

'But you've seen a blue Land Rover?'

'Aye, one or two. Fairly common colour, blue.'

'We're particularly interested in a property with an open stretch at the rear; meadow or grassy area that leads to woods. You know any that fits that description?'

Mills and his wife exchanged glances, then Mrs Mills said, 'Fits Ralph Bellamy's place almost to a tee, don't you think, Davie?'

'Aye, it does,' her husband replied. 'Quiet lad, both he and his wife keep to themselves.'

'Except his wife Nan died at the end of last year, remember?' Mrs Mills said, then turned to McCann. 'We would have gone to the funeral, but a notice in the paper said it was for close relatives only.'

'Mr Bellamy lives on his own?' McCann asked.

'He did do,' Mrs Mills replied. 'Until a few months ago. Alice Cosgrove, an assistant at the Co-op, tells me he's gone to live with his widowed sister in Melrose.'

'So the house is empty?' Hathaway asked.

'As far as I know,' Mrs Mills replied.

'Bellamy's cottage is situated a mile or two from a burn that marks the boundary of my property,' her husband said. 'If it's a clear day, I can see the back end of the house when I'm tending my sheep.' Mr Mills gestured to his wife. 'Christine's right, I haven't seen anyone around lately.'

'But you have in the past?' McCann asked.

'Bellamy himself, no. But occasionally his wife, hanging out washing.'

Mrs Mills made a sign of the cross. 'God bless her soul,' she said.

McCann thanked the couple, then she and Hathaway took their leave.

As they got back into the Astra, Hathaway said, 'Well that's the first of three ruled out. Likely the Taylor property, too, if we go with Duffy's description. That leaves the Bellamy place, which, according to the Mills, fits like a glove. Except of course that it's empty.'

McCann anchored her seatbelt and turned to Hathaway. 'Aye, but is it really?' she said.

Her young colleague gave an acknowledging nod and turned the key in the ignition. 'Only one way to find out.'

* * *

Grossman knocked on Gibson's bedroom door and said, 'Archie?'

'Yes, Clive?' his guest replied.

'I've been keeping a watch from my garage window,' Grossman said. 'Using binoculars. My neighbour's a sheep farmer, and on a good day I can see his back door from there.'

'Aye?' Gibson said.

'Yes,' Grossman replied. 'Thing is, he and his sheepdog usually leave spot on nine to move his flock to upper pasture, a field over the stream near my property. Except this morning. He put the dog in his Land Rover and went back into the house.'

'Sorry, Clive,' Gibson said. 'I'm not with you.'

'His wife called him back in. I think they've got company.'

'Police?' Gibson said.

140

'Yes,' Grossman replied. 'Which means we're next for a visit.'

'Oh, right. How long do you reckon?'

'About ten minutes,' Grossman replied. 'You've got your pyjamas on? The robe I gave you?'

Gibson opened the bedroom door and ran his hand down the lapel of a checked dressing gown. 'Aye, Clive,' he said. 'Ready the moment the bell rings.'

'Good.'

'But, Clive…'

'Yes?'

'What if they expect me to ask them in?'

'Like I said, Archie, you're recovering from a bout of Covid. They'll keep their distance. Won't expect to be asked in. Or want to, come to that.'

'Aye, I suppose you're right.'

Grossman dipped his head in acknowledgement. 'You remember your wife's name?'

Gibson nodded. 'Nan.'

'And when did she die?'

'November 21st, last year.'

'Good,' Grossman said. 'Like I said earlier, Archie, just stick to the script and you'll be fine. Do you want a drink of water before they arrive?'

'Nip of whisky would be better.'

'No, Archie,' Grossman said, looking mildly irritated. 'If they smell alcohol, it'll make them suspicious.'

Gibson gave Grossman an indulgent smile. 'Only joking, son.'

At that moment the men heard the sound of a vehicle coming to a halt on the road outside. Grossman went to the window and glanced out.

'A dark-blue Astra's stopped at the gate,' he said. 'Driver's a man in his thirties, passenger a woman about ten years older. It's them, Archie – are you ready?'

'Aye,' Gibson replied. 'Ready as I'll ever be.'

'Right,' Grossman said. 'I'll be in the kitchen.'

Seconds later the doorbell rang. Gibson ambled to the door, opened it, and saw McCann and Hathaway standing on the step.

'Good morning,' McCann said, showing Gibson her warrant card. 'I'm DS McCann, Edinburgh Police, and this is my colleague, DC Hathaway. We're here in connection with an abducted girl, Olivia Ledbetter. There's reason to believe she's being held somewhere in the area. Would you mind if we asked a couple of questions?'

Gibson held a hand to his mouth and coughed a couple of times. 'No, that's okay,' he said. 'But it'll have to be out here, hen. I can't invite you in – getting over a bout of Covid.'

'Oh, I see,' McCann said. 'You're feeling better now?'

Gibson coughed again. 'A bit,' he replied. 'Wasn't as bad as it might have been. Good job I had the jags.'

'Where were you treated?' McCann asked. 'Here in Newcastleton?'

'Aye, local nurse. Had the jags at East–' Gibson stopped, corrected himself, and said, 'Eastway Street, Hawick.'

McCann waved to their surroundings. 'You're the owner of the property?' she said.

'Yes, I am.'

'What is your name, sir?'

'Bellamy,' Gibson replied. 'Ralph Bellamy.'

McCann pointed back towards Newcastleton. 'The reason I ask is that we've just spoken to your neighbours, Mr and Mrs Mills. They're under the impression you'd gone to live with your sister.'

Gibson shrugged. 'Ah, well,' he said. 'Newcastleton's a small place. Maybe somebody heard me talking to someone. You see, after my wife's funeral I went to stay with my sister for a couple of weeks. She's been after me to sell up and move in permanently. Worries about me being on my own. I'm thinking about it, haven't made up my mind yet.' Gibson covered his mouth and coughed again. 'Sorry,' he said.

McCann nodded. 'Okay,' she said, 'we'll try not to keep you too long.' A pause. 'When you answered the door I was asking about Olivia Ledbetter, the girl who's been missing for almost a week now.'

'Aye,' Gibson said. 'I saw reports on television.'

'We spoke to a man who drove this way yesterday and discovered he had a slow puncture. Claims he approached a young man to ask for help, but was rudely rebuffed.'

'Here?' Gibson said.

'Yes,' McCann said, motioning towards the area next to the cottage. 'The meadow between the cottage and the woods.'

'Couldn't have been,' Gibson said. 'Unless…'

'Yes?' McCann said.

Gibson pointed to a stretch of land opposite. 'A couple of cyclists pitched a tent over there at the weekend, young lad and a girl. Could have been them.'

'What did they look like?'

'The lad was in his mid-twenties, dark-haired, quite athletic-looking. The girl a few years younger. About five-two, blonde.'

'M-hmm,' McCann said. 'How long did they stay?'

'I'm not sure,' Gibson replied. 'I began to feel a bit ropey on Sunday, which is when I took to my bed. Didn't see anyone after that.'

'You saw a nurse?' Hathaway said. 'When was that?'

'Aye, sorry. Monday. I phoned my local GP and the nurse looked in on me in the afternoon. Told me to remain in bed, stay hydrated, and take paracetamol.'

'The car driver we interviewed told us the man had a firm grip on the girl's wrist,' McCann said. 'She broke free, ran for the woods, and he shouted after her. You didn't hear anything?'

'Nope,' Gibson replied and coughed again. 'But like I say, I was in my bed, getting over this.' Gibson gestured to his chest and added, 'I might've been sleeping.'

'The man who remonstrated with the driver claimed that this cottage was his property,' McCann said. 'Why do you think he'd say that?'

'God only knows,' Gibson replied. 'Knew he was on someone's land, maybe, didn't want to alert whoever was in the house?'

'Yes, it could've been that,' McCann said, and took a step back. 'Okay, Mr Bellamy,' she said. 'We'll let you get back inside, and I hope you're better soon. Thanks for talking to us.'

Gibson nodded. 'Aye, you're welcome,' he said, then retreated over the threshold and closed the door.

* * *

'I'm sure I've seen Bellamy somewhere before,' Hathaway was saying. A few minutes had passed and he and McCann were approaching the last of three dwellings on that stretch of the road, the B&B that Sergeant Duffy had told them about.

'Part of the criminal fraternity, you mean?' McCann replied.

'I'm not sure,' Hathaway said. 'Some time back. I'm seeing him as a younger man.'

'How long back?'

'A fair bit. When I was in uniform. Maybe ten or fifteen years.' A pause. 'I took a picture on my iPhone while you were talking to him.'

McCann checked her watch. 'The boss should have arrived by now,' she said. 'You can show him the image when you get back. See if it rings any bells.'

A few moments later they arrived at the B&B where a small bespectacled man answered their knock on the door.

'Mr Charles Taylor?' McCann asked.

'Yes.'

McCann showed him her warrant card, introduced herself and Hathaway, and told him the purpose of their visit. Taylor ushered them inside and showed them around the property.

'Only three guests have stayed with us in the last week,' he explained. 'A middle-aged American couple and a regular; a lad from Middlesborough who's a rep for a cash register company.'

'Sergeant Duffy told us you had outbuildings?' McCann said.

'Aye,' Taylor said. 'Four cabins I had built a couple of years back. Single or double occupancy. They've been empty all winter. I usually only rent them out during the summer months, when it's busier.'

'We think the man who abducted the girl drives a blue Land Rover,' McCann said. 'I know they're fairly common in these parts, but you haven't seen one lately whose driver you didn't recognise?'

'No,' Taylor said. 'Apart from Davie Mills and one or two sheep farmers further up, the road's been quiet.'

'We've just spoken to Ralph Bellamy,' McCann said. 'Your neighbour along the road. 'You don't happen to have seen strangers around his place?'

Taylor shook his head. 'Haven't had cause to head that way for several weeks now,' he said. 'My wife gets odds and ends, perishables like fruit and veg, when she shops in Newcastleton. Aside from that, we're fairly well-stocked. Last time I was in town was the end of March.' Taylor paused. 'I was under the impression Bellamy had gone to stay with his sister in Melrose.'

'Do you recall who told you that?' McCann asked.

'My wife, I think. Wait a minute,' he said, then turned and called out, 'Mary!' Then to McCann, he added, 'Only be a tick, she's in the kitchen.'

A few moments later a small woman wearing a pinafore appeared at the door of the lounge.

'Charlie,' she admonished. 'Why didn't you tell me we had guests?'

'They're detectives, Mary,' Taylor said, 'from Edinburgh. Investigating the case of girl who was abducted. They think she might be in the area.'

'Really?' his wife said. 'Here, in Newcastleton?'

'Yes,' Taylor said. 'They were asking about Ralph Bellamy.'

'Ralph? He's gone to live with his sister, in Melrose.'

'Do you remember who told you that, dear?' Taylor asked.

'Rosie at the Co-op,' Mrs Taylor said, then frowned and added, 'Or was it Alice?' She shook her head. 'One of the two, anyway.'

'I'm Detective Sergeant McCann, Mrs Taylor,' McCann said. 'Your husband tells us you've been going to Newcastleton to top up supplies. Do you drive into town often?'

'Every other day.'

'Mr Bellamy's cottage,' McCann said. 'You haven't seen anyone in or around the property on your journeys to and from town?'

Mrs Taylor shook her head. 'No,' she replied emphatically. 'Not since he went to live with his sister.'

Chapter Twenty-one

'Strange that both of Bellamy's neighbours think he's gone to live with his sister,' Knox was saying. McCann and Hathaway had just got back to Newcastleton Police Station and discovered that Knox had arrived in their absence. Inspector Laing was also in the room, directing his officers' operations via radio.

'Did you see any vehicles in the driveway?' Knox said.

'Only a white Mondeo,' Hathaway replied. 'No sign of a Land Rover. Couldn't make out an index number. The view to the driveway was blocked by plants.'

'Anything unusual about Bellamy?'

'Mark thought he'd seen him before,' McCann said.

'Yes, boss, a while back,' Hathaway said. 'I took a picture while Arlene was interviewing him.'

'Let's have a look.'

Hathaway took out his iPhone, navigated to the photo library, and handed over the device.

Knox studied the image for a moment. 'You're right, Mark,' he said. 'He looks familiar.' He paused and addressed McCann, 'Any indication he wasn't kosher?'

'No. He seemed confident,' McCann replied. 'Wasn't ill at ease or anything. Except…'

'Yes?' Knox said.

'Well, there was one thing. He said he was getting over a bout of Covid, but he'd previously been vaccinated.'

'Yes, go on.'

'When he explained he'd had the jags, he stumbled when he said where he'd been given them. He started to say "East" then caught himself – as though he was going to say somewhere else.'

'Where did he say he was vaccinated?'

'Eastway Street, in Hawick.'

Inspector Laing looked up from his desk and turned down the volume of his radio. 'Eastway Street in Hawick?' he asked.

'Yes, sir,' McCann said.

'There's no such place,' Laing said. 'As far as I know, all Covid inoculations were carried out at Hawick Town Hall, located in Cross Wynd.'

Knox's brow furrowed. He thought for a moment and said, 'Let me see the image again, Mark.'

Hathaway handed over the phone. Knox studied the photo for a second or two, then a thin smile played on his lips. 'Well, well,' he said. 'Archie Gibson. Quite a prolific housebreaker back in the mid-1990s and early 2000s. His hair was darker then; thicker, too. Stays in Montgomery Street.' A pause. 'If I remember correctly, all the Covid vaccinations for that area were given at the Easter Road stadium. That's why he stumbled.'

'But how does he know Grossman?' Hathaway asked.

Knox glanced at his watch. 'That's what I'd like to find out,' he said. 'How long since you talked to him, Arlene?'

McCann thought for a minute. 'We interviewed the Millses first,' she said. 'That took around a half hour. About nine-thirty, I think.'

'Ten-thirty now,' Knox said. 'I'm guessing Grossman bought the cottage from Bellamy and didn't bother updating the property register. After McClure spotted him with Olivia, he knew we'd come calling. He paid Gibson to impersonate Bellamy.'

'I'm betting Gibson will take his leave soon, if he hasn't already,' Knox added, then turned to Laing. 'Dave, could you have your guys look out for a white Mondeo? Elderly driver the only occupant. No index number, but it can't be hard to find. Check the town and the B6357 between here and Hawick. Have them arrest him and bring him here, will you?'

Laing reached for his radio. 'Sure thing, Jack,' he replied.

* * *

'It was my stutter over the Covid jags that gave me away, wasn't it?' Archie Gibson was saying. He was sitting opposite Knox and McCann in a small interview room at the rear of Newcastleton Police Station. Two of Laing's patrol officers had intercepted his Mondeo at the corner of Langholm Street and the B6357 half an hour earlier.

'That and the fact that it's common knowledge that the real Mr Bellamy has gone to Melrose to live with his sister,' Knox replied.

Gibson shrugged. 'So, what am I guilty of? Grossman paid me to pretend to be Bellamy to put you off the scent. To allow him and his fiancée to start a new life in peace, without interference from her domineering father.'

'Grossman told you that?' McCann asked.

'Aye. He said her old man was a tyrant. That she was afraid he would force her to follow a career in law, against her wishes.'

'You're aware that Grossman abducted Olivia forcibly, aren't you?' Knox said. 'You couldn't have missed it. It's been all over the media in the last week.'

'Aye, of course. But it was flannel. Clive said the girl wanted to be with him and they'd eloped together. He told me it was her father who put out the abduction story. Clive bought the cottage because it was secluded and they could start a new life, away from his influence.'

'You really believe that?' Knox asked.

'Don't see any reason not to.' Gibson frowned. 'Why, are you telling me the abduction story is real?'

Knox ignored the question. 'Did you see Olivia, Mr Gibson?' he said.

'No,' Gibson replied. 'Clive told me she had suffered some kind of mental breakdown at the thought of her father discovering her whereabouts, and became distraught. Clive's a chemist – he gave her a sedative to ease her agitation and to help her sleep.' He studied the detectives' impassive expressions for a moment, then the penny dropped. 'Oh, my God; he's conned me, hasn't he?'

Again Knox ignored the question. 'How much did he pay you, Mr Gibson?'

'A grand,' Gibson replied.

'And you really expect us to accept that you believed she'd gone with him willingly?' Knox said. 'You were in it from the start, weren't you? You do appreciate how serious this is? You're facing a charge of aiding and abetting the perpetration of a crime.'

'Now, hold on a minute,' Gibson said. 'I may have been a wee bit naïve, but I honestly didn't…' Gibson blanched. 'Oh, Christ, I'm in the shit, aren't I?'

'How did you meet Grossman?' Knox asked.

Gibson explained he'd first seen him in Middleton's in January, where Grossman said he'd just bought a place in Edina Street. Gibson had helped him decorate the flat, and when the work was finished had given him his card and told Grossman to get in touch if he was needed again.

'He knew you had a criminal record?'

'I told him, yes.'

'When did he phone to ask if you'd come to Newcastleton?' Knox asked.

'Yesterday.'

'You didn't stop to think his offer of a thousand pounds was a bit suspicious?'

'I can see that now,' Gibson replied. 'But at the time…'

'Okay,' Knox said. 'I'm going to ask you a series of questions regarding the layout of the cottage – where Olivia's bedroom is located, that sort of thing. If you cooperate fully, I'll make sure the procurator fiscal knows, which will count in your favour when your case comes to court. I take it you're okay with that?'

Gibson nodded emphatically. 'Of course,' he said.

* * *

The convoy stopped around five hundred yards from Grossman's property. This part of the road was screened by a line of birch trees, and could not be seen from the cottage.

Knox's Passat was the lead vehicle, followed by Inspector Laing's Vectra and a divisional Transit van with six officers. Hathaway's Astra brought up the rear, joined by an ambulance from Hawick Community Hospital. Officers in the first three vehicles exited, and Laing ordered four men to take to the grassland on the other side of the trees and advance stealthily towards the back of the cottage. Meanwhile he, Knox, Fulton and the other two officers made for the front using the hedges and a low wall for cover.

Two uniformed policemen – one of the four making for the rear, and one of the two with Knox – carried a Sigma battering ram, known colloquially as "The Big Red Key", to force entry at a prearranged signal.

Knox and his group covered the final twenty yards in a crab-like crawl, then Laing turned down the volume of his radio, thumbed the transmit button, and spoke into the mic. 'Officers at the rear – confirm you're in position, over.'

The radio crackled and a barely audible voice replied, 'In position, sir.'

'Okay,' Laing said. 'Go on my signal. Acknowledge.'

'Understood, sir,' came the reply. 'We go on your signal.'

'Okay,' Laing said. 'Stand by.' He turned to Knox. 'You're going to phone him first?'

'Yes,' Knox replied. 'On his mobile. He rang Gibson yesterday, who gave me his number. It's likely Grossman will be in or near the bedroom at the rear, where Olivia's being held. He might let his landline go unanswered – but I don't think his iPhone.' A pause. 'Your guys know where the bedroom is located?'

'All thoroughly briefed, Jack,' Laing said. 'They'll make a beeline for it the moment they enter, as will we. The first men there will neutralise Grossman. We're aware that's the priority.'

'Okay,' Knox said, then switched his mobile to speaker-mode, highlighted the number and tapped *call*.

A few seconds later Grossman answered, 'Hello?'

'Clive Grossman?' Knox said. 'This is Inspector Knox, Edinburgh Police. We know you have Olivia in the house, and also where she's located. The cottage is surrounded. I want you to do yourself a favour and give yourself up.'

A short silence, then, 'You said your name was Knox?'

'Yes.'

'I take it you arrested Gibson?'

'Yes,' Knox replied.

'I expect he gave you the layout of the house?'

'Yes,' Knox replied. 'Yes, he did.'

'You say he told you where Olivia is?'

'Yes.'

'Well, what Gibson couldn't have told you is that Olivia is in bed, unconscious, and has a cannula in her left arm. You know what a cannula is, Knox?'

'Yes,' Knox replied. 'I know what a cannula is.'

'To make it easier to administer drugs directly into a vein, right?'

Knox ignored the question. 'You have drugs, Mr Grossman?'

'Oh, yes, Knox, I have drugs.' A pause. 'You've heard of ketamine?'

'Yes, Mr Grossman. I've heard of ketamine.'

'Then you'll have a good idea why Olivia is presently unconscious.'

'She was unconscious when Mr Gibson arrived yesterday?'

'She was. Why?'

'Because you've given her a fair amount over the last couple of days – with a potential for overdose. I'd like her to see a doctor. I say again, Mr Grossman, for Olivia's sake, give yourself up.'

'The last time I spoke to Olivia,' Grossman replied, 'I told her if there was any danger of her being taken away from me, I wouldn't allow it.' A pause. 'You know about my having ketamine. Which means you'll know I have another drug, too, which is fatal. Pentobarbital takes a half minute to work, and I have two hypodermics set up and ready. One for Olivia, another for me.'

Grossman continued, 'You said you had the cottage surrounded, Knox. No doubt you intend forcing your way in. I just want to let you know I'm about to administer the drug. We'll be gone before you get to us.'

'Before you do,' Knox said. 'You should know I had a call this morning from G&R Pharmaceuticals. I spoke to your ex-boss, Mr Medwin.'

'Then you'll know I'm telling the truth,' Grossman said.

'On the contrary, Mr Grossman. It appears there's been some sort of mix-up. It wasn't pentobarbital you took, it was phenobarbital. Seems the warehouseman stored the drugs in the wrong place.'

Again, they heard movement over the iPhone's speaker. Knox guessed Grossman had gone to check the labelling. A moment later they heard a shout of anger when he realised what Knox said had been true.

'Bastard!' Grossman exclaimed.

Knox nodded to Laing, who pressed the transmit button. 'Go, go, go!' he said.

A few seconds passed, and the officer with the Sigma was at the door, smashing his way in. Meanwhile, the sound of splintering wood came from the opposite side of the house.

As Knox entered, he saw two officers had already gained entry from the rear, and witnessed a flash of uniforms as the men jinked around the hallway on their way to the back bedroom. A hefty shoulder connected with the door, and the policemen were inside.

One moment Grossman was standing at a dressing table with the phenobarbital bottle in his hand; the next he'd been wrestled to the floor. There the policemen pinned his arms behind his back, while a third officer – one of the men who'd entered with Laing – snapped handcuffs on his wrists.

Knox looked to the bed, where Olivia lay, oblivious to the commotion.

He turned to Fulton. 'Go back to where the vehicles are parked, Bill, and get the doctor. He's with Mark and Arlene in the Astra. Have the ambulance come up, too.'

'Boss.'

Chapter Twenty-two

Thirty minutes later, Grossman had been charged and bundled off in the divisional Transit van. The doctor checked Olivia and determined it was likely she was suffering from an overdose of ketamine, and that a gastrointestinal detox might be necessary. She was taken to Newcastleton and an air ambulance was summoned to pick her up at the town's Douglas Square for transfer to Edinburgh Royal Infirmary.

Knox and his team bagged and tagged the evidence, including Grossman's drugs and syringes, and returned to Newcastleton with Laing. As they watched the helicopter take off, Knox turned to the Hawick inspector.

'I'd like to thank you and your lads for taking down Grossman so quickly, Dave,' Knox said, nodding to the helicopter, which had now cleared the landing site and was pulling away from the town. 'If he'd managed to give her phenobarbital on top of ketamine, she just might not have made it.'

'Thanks, Jack; it was a near thing. Even though I had every faith in them, I'm glad my men were up to it. I'll be more than happy to pass on your thanks.'

Knox shook Laing's hand and glanced at his watch. 'Well, we better get going. It's been a pleasure working with you.'

'Any time, Jack,' Laing replied, then smiled and added, 'but not too soon, eh?'

* * *

'I've just taken a call from Alan Moodie,' Warburton was saying. 'He told me to pass on his thanks for collaring Grossman and freeing Ms Ledbetter.'

Knox and his team had arrived back at Gayfield Square in the early afternoon and the DCI had joined them in the main office.

'How is Olivia?' Knox asked. 'Did the ACC say?'

'Out of assessment and taken up to one of the main wards,' Warburton replied. 'I'm told she was sitting up, talking to her parents.'

Knox dipped his head in acknowledgement. 'Glad everything worked out okay.'

Warburton nodded. 'The Leckie case,' he said. 'That's tied up, too?'

'Not quite,' Knox replied. 'One or two elements I'm not quite sure about.'

'Really? I thought McVey had been charged and was being held on remand?'

'Yes, sir, he is,' Knox said. 'Bill and I will be heading up to Saughton this afternoon to iron it out. DS McCann and DC Hathaway will remain here meantime; to hold the fort in case anything comes in.'

'Okay, Jack,' Warburton replied. 'But let me know how you get on before you leave for the night, okay?'

'Will do, sir,' Knox replied.

* * *

Ronnie McVey was lying on the bottom bunk of a single occupancy cell in Saughton Prison's remand wing when his attention was drawn to the door. A key turned in the lock, the door opened, and a prison officer stood facing him.

'Shoes on, McVey,' the man said. 'And follow me. You've got a visitor.'

'A visitor?' McVey said as he levered himself into a sitting position and put on a pair of slip-ons. 'Who is it, boss?'

'They don't tell me everything, son,' the officer said. 'Only that you've got a visitor.'

McVey followed the officer along a series of corridors, then the man stopped and pointed to a door. 'In there, McVey,' he said. 'It's an ante-room. Take a seat and another officer will call you.'

McVey entered the room, which was empty save for a row of chairs. He took a seat and had barely settled when a second officer entered from a door opposite and beckoned to him.

'Ms Lorna Telford to see you, McVey,' he said. 'Special visit.' A pause. 'I take it she's your girlfriend?'

'Fiancée, boss.'

'Well, you have fifteen minutes and I have to remain in the room with you. You're allowed an embrace at the start and when the visit is over, but only then. You understand?'

'Yes, boss.'

'Okay. This way.'

McVey followed him into the room, which, like the ante-room, was empty except for a medium-size table and two chairs, one placed at either side.

Lorna was sitting on the chair farthest away, facing him. The moment he entered, her face lit up and she flashed him a broad smile.

'Ronnie,' she said opening her arms to embrace him.

McVey went to the side of the table and took her in his arms. 'My dad phoned?' he said.

'Yes,' she replied. 'Asked me to come over, said he had some good news and some bad news.'

The prison officer, who had taken up position at a wall opposite, cleared his throat. McVey looked towards him, and the man made a gesture indicating they should sit.

'Better take a seat, Lorna,' McVey said.

Telford glanced at the officer. 'Oh, yes,' she said. 'Sorry.' Then she turned to McVey. 'You're okay?'

'Fine, Lorna, fine. What did Dad say?'

'That you've been charged with shooting four men in Edinburgh, Ronnie. Is that true?'

McVey glanced at the prison officer again. 'We've not got all that much time, sweetheart,' he said. 'But yes, it's true. Four men who abused me as a kid. I'll explain later.'

'But you *have* been charged?'

'Yes, but it's not as bad as it sounds. Mitigating circumstances, my brief says. Culpable homicide, not murder. Thinks I'll get five years, be out in three.'

Lorna took a hankie from her handbag and dabbed her eyes. 'Oh, Ronnie, darling, I'm sorry. I wish you'd told me.'

'Didn't want to upset you, did I?' McVey smiled and leaned forward. 'Now, let's talk about the good news. Dad gave you something?'

'Oh, Ronnie, darling, yes; the ring. It's gorgeous.'

'You were surprised?'

Telford gave a coquettish smile. 'Well, we'd talked about it but, yes, I guess I was a little.'

'But I'd asked you to marry me, hadn't I?' McVey said.

'I know, but–'

'There you go, then. Had to do the honours. Make it official, like.'

Telford sniffed, brightened a little, and opened her handbag. She put the hankie away, and took out an oblong box inlaid with gold scrollwork. She snapped it open to reveal a gold ring inset with a sparkling gemstone.

'The jeweller says it's only moissanite, Lorna,' McVey said. 'Not a diamond. But I promise you, once I've served my time, you'll have a solid gold ring at our wedding. You'll wait for me?'

'But, Ronnie, it's beautiful,' Telford said, then looked directly into his eyes, and added, 'Of course I will.'

McVey nodded towards the box. 'Put on the ring, see if it fits.'

Telford smiled. 'I already have, darling. I tried it on, on the way here. It fits perfectly.'

'Then put it on now, sweetheart,' McVey said.

Telford slid the ring onto her middle finger and gave a little smile. 'There you are; like I said, a perfect fit.'

McVey nodded towards the box. 'You'll keep the box, too,' he said. 'Even though you're wearing the ring?'

'Of course I will, darling,' his fiancée said. 'Why should I do otherwise?'

'Just that both ring and box complement each other. It'll make an attractive keepsake in years to come.'

The prison officer checked his watch at that moment and cleared his throat again. 'Sorry, folks,' he said. 'Time's up.' He turned to Telford and added, 'Sorry, miss, I'll have to ask you to leave.'

Telford and McVey stood and embraced again. 'Visits are allowed three times a week while I'm on remand, Lorna,' McVey said. 'Mondays, Wednesdays and Fridays.'

His fiancée kissed him on the lips. 'Then I'll see you on Monday, darling,' she said. 'Remember – I love you.'

'You, too, Lorna,' McVey replied. 'See you on Monday.'

* * *

McVey was reading a magazine left by a previous occupant when the prison officer returned. 'You're a popular man, McVey,' he said. 'You've another visitor.'

McVey put down the magazine and got to his feet. 'Who, boss?'

'Like I said last time, son, they don't tell me.' A pause. 'Come on; same place.'

McVey followed the officer, who escorted him to the room where he'd been previously. McVey entered and was ushered inside, but this time there were two chairs on the other side of the table, behind which Knox and Fulton were seated. A NEAL recording machine had been placed near Knox's elbow.

Knox waved to the remaining chair. 'Take a seat, Mr McVey, please,' he said, and switched on the recorder. 'Second interview with Ronald McVey at HMP Edinburgh,' he said. 'Today's date is April 20. Time 3.47pm. Present in the room are the prisoner, myself, DI Knox, and my colleague, DS Fulton.'

'I don't understand,' McVey said. 'You took my statement at Gayfield Square.'

'One or two factors have come to light, Mr McVey,' Knox said, 'which need clarification.'

'What factors?'

Knox ignored the question. 'We crossed paths with your fiancée, Lorna Telford, on our way in.'

'Aye?' McVey said.

'I asked if she'd mind speaking to us for a moment and she agreed. I told her I was surprised to see her, as I was under the impression she'd broken off the engagement.'

'I didn't say–' McVey began.

'You told us you had an argument in Prestonpans High Street, didn't you?' Knox said. 'Ms Telford refuted it. She told us that your father phoned and asked to see her last night. He broke the news that you'd been arrested and gave her the ring. He told her you'd phoned late yesterday afternoon, from here.'

'Yes,' McVey said. 'I said the ring was in a chest of drawers in my bedroom and asked him to give it to her. I told the warden afterwards that I was engaged, asked if I could have a special visit on compassionate grounds. He said he'd give it consideration. I was taken aback when she visited today. Didn't expect he'd allow it so soon.'

'So you agree you made a false statement yesterday? You didn't have an argument with Ms Telford in Prestonpans High Street?'

McVey shrugged his shoulders. 'I may have exaggerated a little.'

Knox gave McVey a pointed look. 'To make your assault story all the more convincing?'

'Now wait a minute–' McVey said.

'We checked, Mr McVey,' Knox interrupted. 'There's only one knitwear firm in Peebles – Lyle & Mackie Woollens. Joan Leckie worked there from August 1996 until shortly before her death in January 2003. At no time did she work shifts. Ms Gavin, the personnel manager, tells us the latest Mrs Leckie finished was 4pm.'

'It's a really long time ago,' McVey said. 'And I was stressed, as you might imagine. Maybe she was out shopping when the assaults took place.'

'You expect us to believe the alleged assaults happened while she was shopping?' Knox said. 'That Leckie rang Copeley, Reilly and Scott and had them come up, with the possibility that his wife might return at any moment?' He paused. 'Sorry, Mr McVey, that just won't wash.'

Knox fished in his pocket, took out a key, and placed it on the table. 'The key to box 518 at CincScot Security, George Street,' he said. 'We checked that too, and discovered Leckie had an account with the company dating back to 2001, two years before he and the others – including your father – carried out the raid. We're guessing Leckie transferred the diamonds from box 535 at the height of the job, and the others didn't notice.'

McVey pointed to the key. 'Where did you get it?' he said.

'Where you put it,' Knox replied. 'Underneath the ring pillow in the box you had your father give Lorna.'

'But how–'

'How did we know where it was?' Knox said. 'Well, the fact is, we didn't. As I told you, when we asked Lorna about the break-up and she denied it, she showed us the ring on her finger, then took the box from her handbag and was about to show us that, too. Unfortunately, it slipped out of her hands and the key popped out of its hiding place. I retrieved the box and palmed the key. I replaced the ring pillow, and returned it to her.'

'Aye,' Fulton said. 'The lassie made quite a fuss of examining the box, too, to check if it had been damaged. Told us you'd asked her to take special care of it, eh, Mr McVey? A "special keepsake", she said you'd called it. Now we understand why.'

McVey remained silent for a long moment, then placed his hands palm down on the table and emitted an audible sigh. 'Okay,' he said, 'but Leckie deserved everything he got.'

'Deserved?' Knox said. 'How?'

'Not only did he cheat my father, he treated him like dirt. Dad had partnered him in the robbery, contributed more than the others. Yet when he ran into him in the high street soon after his release, Leckie ignored him.'

'Your father told us Leckie offered him a job,' Knox said.

McVey made a face. 'Aye, as some kind of gopher like the three at Spylaw? Paying sweeties? Nah, Leckie could have done better than that. He and Dad were supposed to be mates, they knew each other since their twenties. Then, when my dad had his accident a few months later, Leckie ignored him – not a phone call, a card, nothing. Don't get me wrong, Dad wasn't bitter about it – hardly mentioned it, in fact. But some nights when he'd had a few beers, he'd bring it up. I knew it still irked him.'

'He knew about the missing jewels?' Knox said.

'Yeah, he mentioned them once or twice.'

'When did you decide to do something about it?'

'Soon after January, 2020, when the effects of Brexit started to kick in. Courier drivers faced a mountain of paperwork if they wanted to continue working in Europe. That and five-mile queues at Dover. I decided to go on the parcels – delivering door-to-door for online companies. Not the same, though; I saw a fair-sized drop in income.'

'Then you remembered Leckie's jewels?' Fulton said.

McVey shrugged his shoulders. 'Yeah, a few months ago Dad and I had a few beers and he brought it up again. Then I got to thinking…'

'What you told us about stalking Leckie, that was true?' Knox asked.

'Yeah, pretty much.'

'The three men you shot in cold blood,' Fulton said. 'Just collateral damage?'

'They were petty crooks, like Leckie,' McVey said venomously.

'And had to be out of the way if your assault alibi was to work?'

McVey shook his head. 'I'm not stupid,' he said. 'I knew DNA would put me in the frame sooner or later. I had to think of a way to get a lesser sentence.'

'Well, Mr McVey,' Knox said. 'Seems your plan didn't work as intended.' He nodded to the recording machine and added, 'Your statement will be forwarded to the procurator fiscal with a revised charge of murder.'

The detectives stood and Fulton knocked on the door, The prison officer entered and addressed Knox. 'Interview over, sir?'

'Yes,' Knox replied. 'Interview over.'

* * *

The detectives returned to Gayfield Square where Knox updated Warburton. 'He confessed?' the DCI asked.

'Yes, sir,' Knox said. 'We've got it all on tape.'

'What made you suspect him?'

'I thought it strange that Leckie's wife would leave a seven-year-old child with her husband. Then go to work having made a promise to look after him while his mother was in hospital. She'd be more likely to take a couple of nights off. So I phoned the firm…'

'And discovered Leckie's wife would have been at home?'

'Yes, sir. But the really important piece of luck was intercepting McVey's fiancée and finding the key.'

'Indeed,' Warburton agreed. 'A happy accident.'

'Yes, sir.'

Warburton consulted his watch. 'Well, it's almost six. If there's nothing else, I suppose we can wrap up.'

'Sir.'

Knox left Warburton's office and went back to where the others were. 'Okay,' he said, 'we can call it a day.' He turned to McCann and Hathaway. 'I appreciate your work on the Ledbetter case, Arlene and Mark. I was asked to pass on the ACC's thanks.'

'No problem, boss.' McCann said, then winked. 'Matter of fact, it wasn't all that bad. My room in the Elm House had a mini bar. I partook of a couple of Gordons with a squeeze of lemon.'

Knox grinned. 'And you, Mark. What did you find in the mini bar?'

Hathaway hung his head. 'The only thing in mine was orange juice.'

Warburton exited his office at that moment, and the Major Incident Inquiry room erupted with laughter.

'Don't mind me,' he said as he approached the exit door. 'Nice to know I've a happy crew, though.'

* * *

Knox checked his watch. Three minutes after six, and the roads were still thick with homeward commuters. He had a choice of driving via Abbeyhill and Holyrood Park, or the North and South Bridges. A long column of slow-moving vehicles were backed up on Leith Street, so he decided to go via the park.

He passed Abbeyhill and drove through Horse Wynd, past a knot of tourists on his left taking photographs of Holyrood Palace. On his right, a small group of protesters with placards were picketing the entrance to the Scottish Parliament.

His mobile rang at that moment. He removed it from his pocket, placed it on the dash, and switched to speakers. He glanced at the screen and tapped *accept*.

'Hello, Lucy,' he said. 'Thought you were in the States?'

'Got back a few days early,' Carmichael said.

'Where are you?'

'Coming in from the airport. My taxi's on the bypass. I fancy a drink, thought I'd stop off at a little wine shop in Morningside. Wondered if you'd care to join me.' A pause. 'I take it you're finished for the day?'

'Just,' Knox replied. 'You've eaten?'

'No, as a matter of fact I'm quite famished.'

'You like curry?'

'Yes. But not too hot.'

'There's a place in St Leonards Street. Hot, but I can have them dial it down a little.'

'What's the dish?'

'Their tandoori chicken's superb. Or vindaloo, if you fancy pork.'

'The Tandoori, I think. What wine goes with it?'

'Don't know,' Knox said. 'I usually have lager.'

'Oh, Jack,' Carmichael said, 'you're such a philistine.'

'I've heard pinot noir's a fair match.'

'I'll ask, get the shop's opinion.'

'Okay,' Knox said. 'Your place or mine?'

'I'm easy.' Carmichael said.

'Oh, I wouldn't say that.'

A loud laugh came through the speakers. 'You're naughty, Jack. You know that?' A pause. 'Thing is, I've a medium-size case and a coat bag, I was wondering if I should drop them off at Ratcliffe Terrace first.'

'You can bring them to mine,' Knox said. 'We can take them round later.'

'That depends,' Carmichael said.

'On what?'

'What brand of toothpaste you use.'

'Colgate Total.'

'That settles it. I'll bring them to yours.'

'And how exactly did you arrive at that decision?'

'I brush my teeth with Corsodyl. I may need it in the morning.'

* * *

Six weeks later Ronald McVey stood in the dock at the High Court of Justiciary at the Supreme Court of Scotland, where he faced the Honourable Mr Justice Parsons. McVey had an indifferent look on his face as the judge said, 'The accused will stand.'

Two police officers flanking McVey nudged him, and all three got to their feet.

'Mr McVey,' the judge said in a sonorous tone. 'You have been found guilty of a most heinous crime, the commission of which was motivated by nothing other than greed – the murders of four men. In carrying out these crimes you not only needlessly brought to an end the life of the person who had in his possession the key that was the passport to the fortune you sought, but you also fabricated a story of abuse at the hands of that man and his employees – three innocent parties whose lives you ended to lend credence to that story.

'This you did to make the police believe you were a victim, when in fact the real victims were the men you shot and killed in cold blood. I have to emphasise that this was a cold, callous and premeditated act. The sentence I am about to hand down, therefore, will reflect the seriousness of that act.

'I hereby sentence you to serve twenty-five years, and release on licence prior to that term being served in full is not recommended.'

McVey stood grim-faced as the policemen took his arms and prepared to remove him from the dock, before Mr Justice Parsons finally declared, 'Take him down.'

End

List of characters

Officers based in Edinburgh

Detective Inspector Jack Knox – head of the Major Incident Inquiry Team based at Gayfield Square Police Station, Edinburgh
Detective Sergeant Bill Fulton – Knox's partner, second member of the Major Incident Inquiry Team
Detective Sergeant Arlene McCann – third member of the Major Incident Inquiry Team
Detective Constable Mark Hathaway – fourth member of the Major Incident Inquiry Team
Detective Chief Inspector Ronald Warburton – senior detective at Gayfield Square Police Station
Detective Inspector Edward (Ed) Murray – forensics officer based in Edinburgh
Detective Sergeant Elizabeth (Liz) Beattie – forensics officer and Murray's assistant

Others

Alexander Turley – pathologist
Lucy Carmichael – pathologist

Assistant Chief Constable Alan Moodie – Police Scotland HQ, Gartcosh
Inspector Dave Laing – Hawick Police
Police Sergeant Niall Duffy – Newcastleton Police
Olivia Ledbetter – abductee
Marcus Ledbetter – Olivia's father
Eloise Ledbetter – Olivia's mother
Fiona Douglas – Olivia's flatmate
Hugh (Shug) Leckie – member of George St heist gang
Andy O'Dowd — member of George St heist gang
Charlie O'Dowd – member of George St heist gang
Thomas Salter – member of George St heist gang
Norman McVey – member of George St heist gang
William Copeley – Leckie's employee
Thomas Reilly – Leckie's employee
Robert Scott – Leckie's employee
Clive Grossman – Olivia's abductor
Ronald (Ronnie) McVey – Norman McVey's son
Lorna Telford – Ronnie's fiancée
Wendy MacDonald – Olivia's colleague
Colin Medwin – manager, G&R Pharmaceuticals
Kirsty Johnson – Leckie's secretary
Frankie Reynolds – Leckie's errand boy
John Coulter – Hawick garage mechanic and foreman
Archie Gibson – Grossman's painter and decorator
Malkie Bowman – apprentice mechanic in Hawick
Thomas McClure – Ferrari driver interviewed by DS McCann
David Mills – Grossman's Newcastleton neighbour
Mrs Annie Mills – David Mills' wife
Mr Charles Taylor – Grossman's other neighbour
Mrs Mary Taylor – Charles Taylor's wife

If you enjoyed this book, please let others know by leaving
a quick review on Amazon. Also, if you spot anything
untoward in the paperback, get in touch. We strive for the
best quality and appreciate reader feedback.

editor@thebookfolks.com

www.thebookfolks.com

MORE FICTION BY ROBERT McNEILL

All the books in this series of DI Jack Knox detective novels are free on Kindle Unlimited and available in paperback!

The Innocent and the Dead (Book 1)

One girl is found dead – strangled in the woods. Another, the daughter of a rich, well-connected businessman, is kidnapped. Unassuming detective Jack Knox must solve these two cases. But the Edinburgh crime-solver will have a hard time getting his superiors to accept his unconventional methods. Will he gamble too much?

Murder at Flood Tide (Book 2)

When a young woman's body is found, the nature of her killing leads detectives to believe the murderer may strike again soon. The race is on to find him, but he has covered his tracks well. DI Jack Knox's investigation is impeded by a disgruntled officer from another force. Can he solve the case and collar the culprit?

Dead of Night (Book 3)

When a philandering French college lecturer is killed and unceremoniously dumped in a canal, DI Jack Knox soon discovers there is no shortage of spurned lovers and jealous husbands who might have done it. He sets about collaring the culprit, but will his efforts be thwarted by unfair complaints made about the investigation?

Noughts and Crosses (Book 4)

After defrauding wealthy investors of a serious amount of money, a financial advisor is found dead on a residential street in Edinburgh. DI Jack Knox must tread carefully to follow the trail that might lead to the killer. But will the events that ensue prove too much even for him?

A View to Murder (Book 5)

When a student is found dead in the crags in Holyrood Park, DI Jack Knox must make sense of her friends' conflicting stories about the events that led up to her death. But his boss risks putting a spanner in the works when Knox is asked to act as a go-between in a deadly drugs sting.

Confession to Murder (Book 6)

After a man confesses in church that he has killed a girl, having wrangled with his conscience the priest tells the police. It would be easy for them to dismiss the confessor as a crank, but DI Knox has a hunch the victim could be a young Canadian tourist who has gone missing. Yet with few other leads, it will take brilliant detective work to catch the killer.

OTHER TITLES OF INTEREST

BRIGHT SPARKS by Traude Ailinger

The death of a local businesswoman in a house fire has
grumpy detective Russell McCord running around in
circles looking for the culprit. Sassy journalist Amy
Thornton has some ideas of her own. But when the smoke
has cleared, can the two crime-solvers put their differences
aside and their heads together to work out the truth?

Available free with Kindle Unlimited and in paperback!

MURDER ON A YORKSHIRE MOOR by Ric Brady

Ex-detective Henry Ward is settling awkwardly into retirement in a quiet corner of Yorkshire when during a walk on the moor he stumbles upon the body of a young man. Suspecting foul play and somewhat relishing the return to a bit of detective work, he resolves to find out who killed him. But will the local force appreciate him sticking his nose in?

Available free with Kindle Unlimited and in paperback!

www.thebookfolks.com

www.ingramcontent.com/pod-product-compliance
Lightning Source LLC
Chambersburg PA
CBHW030956210726
48290CB00007B/2338